FOR THE LOVE OF A BOSS

C.D. Blue

**Lock Down Publications and Ca$h
Presents**

FOR THE LOVE OF A BOSS

A Novel by *C.D. Blue*

For the Love of a Boss

Lock Down Publications
P.O. Box 944
Stockbridge, Ga 30281
www.lockdownpublications.com

Copyright 2021 C.D. Blue
For the Love of a Boss

First Edition March 2021
Printed in the United States of America

This is a work of fiction. Names, characters, places, and incidents either are products of the author's imagination or are used fictitiously. Any similarity to actual events or locales or persons, living or dead, is entirely coincidental.

Lock Down Publications
Like our page on Facebook: Lock Down Publications @
www.facebook.com/lockdownpublications.ldp
Cover design and layout by: **Dynasty Cover Me**
Book interior design by: **Shawn Walker**
Edited by: **Nuel Uyi**

C.D. Blue

Stay Connected with Us!

Text **LOCKDOWN** to 22828 to stay up-to-date with new releases, sneak peaks, contests and more...

Thank you!

Submission Guideline.

Submit the first three chapters of your completed manuscript to ldpsubmissions@gmail.com, subject line: Your book's title. The manuscript must be in a .doc file and sent as an attachment. Document should be in Times New Roman, double spaced and in size 12 font. Also, provide your synopsis and full contact information. If sending multiple submissions, they must each be in a separate email.

Have a story but no way to send it electronically? You can still submit to LDP/Ca$h Presents. Send in the first three chapters, written or typed, of your completed manuscript to:

LDP: Submissions Dept
P.O. Box 944
Stockbridge, Ga 30281

DO NOT send original manuscript. Must be a duplicate.

Provide your synopsis and a cover letter containing your full contact information.

Thanks for considering LDP and Ca$h Presents.

C.D. Blue

Dedication

This series is dedicated to my dad, E. Dawson, Sr. and also Roger
"Rod" Johnson.
Both gone but never forgotten.

Acknowledgements

I want to thank God for all that has been given and forgiven. My
family for their support and my readers for their patience. Thank
you to the people who entered, stayed in my life and for those who
left. Without you, this book would not have been possible. I
appreciate all the memories, good and bad.

A special acknowledgement about Roger "Rod" Johnson. We
always thought you'd still be here with us. Your death impacted
our folk's history, tremendously. I tried my best to capture the
essence of YOU. You are still remembered.

A special thanks to Lock Down Publications' CEO, CA$H. Thank
you for giving me this opportunity and for your much needed
wisdom. I have learned so much working with you and look
forward to learning even more. You are truly appreciated.

For the Love of a Boss

"Man, we were so young! Having fun, thinking the good times, the feelings, the vibes, and the people would stay. We knew we would grow older, get mature; we just didn't know emotions are interchangeable, the energy doesn't stay the same, and that everybody wasn't going with us. When certain bonds are created, the sentiments might be different, people may leave, but the heart never forgets."

Kalissa

C.D. Blue

For the Love of a Boss

PROLOGUE

The club was lit! People were filing in, some dressed to impress; others were simply dressed. The Flight was showcasing a local rap group in Montgomery, Alabama and there had been so much buzz about it. Everybody showed up.

Nigel and Kalissa walked in as though they were royalty. The DJ played "Wait (The Whisper Song)" by the Ying Yang Twins. Nigel danced, creating a walkway and Kalissa followed suit. Getting in front of him, they moved in sync from left to right. Stopping to make some low moves, he grabbed her hips as if they had rehearsed. Their dancing was so smooth people parted like the Red Sea.

Nigel and Kalissa didn't half step; they were the best-looking couple there. Nigel had on a brown casual Fendi jacket and slacks with a gold tee shirt, looking good, with Kalissa on his arm. She wore a gold sequined dress that barely covered her little ass. Her hair hung down her back. She smiled 'cause the hoes were casting looks of pure hatred at her while the men were panting. Just the way she liked it.

"You want something to drink?" Nigel was close by.

From the moment they got out of the car, he kept her in his grip. This was their first time out clubbing. As fine as he looked, she was amenable to his charms. Turning to look into his brown eyes, she wanted to fuck him right there. This man had her dickmatized and she was not ashamed to admit it.

"Yeah, get me a beer."

"Naw, baby. You can drink beer at home. Out here you need some liquor. I'll get you something after I find us a table. I see I need to put you in a corner somewhere before I have to bust one of these niggas upside the head for looking too hard."

A voice in the back of Kalissa's head wondered how the hell he thought he could tell her what to drink but she giggled aloud. "In Da Club" by 50 Cent was blaring through the speakers as Nigel continued to lead her dancing to the back of the club, stopping every five seconds to speak to someone. His cousin, Rod, trailed behind them, quiet as usual.

Once they sat down, Nigel headed to the bar, leaving her and Rod alone. Of all his friends and family, Rod was the only one she could tolerate. He was about his business and had sense. The rest of them just seemed to be bum ass niggas.

With a swift glance around, she saw big ballers, little ballers, small change, and a few bums. She could tell who was balling 'cause they had the thirstiest hoes hanging around. One dark-skinned guy, who looked slightly familiar, lifted his drink in the air to her. Wearing a ton of gold around his neck, arm and on his fingers, she knew he was a big baller. The woman with him looked in Kalissa's direction and scowled. Kalissa stared back with her head cocked to the side, never wavering.

"Who you mean-mugging?" Nigel laughed as he approached with the drinks.

"Nobody. What you bring me?" Her scowl immediately turned into a smile.

"Some Henny, 'cause when we get back to your place I'ma make you cluck," Nigel said, before he leaned over and licked her face.

Blushing, she rolled her eyes.

"I see yo' boy is here, too," Nigel said over the music.

"Who?"

He grimaced as he took a swig of his drink. She took one swallow of her own drink, the Hennessy burning her throat. The only person she considered to be 'her boy' was Taj; she knew he wasn't at the club. When Nigel didn't answer, she bobbed her head to the music.

"Hey! What up?" A woman with a red weave and blue contacts slid in Nigel's face.

"What up? Do I know you?" He waved her off.

"Oh, so it's like that? Humph, I see," she shot back, looking at Kalissa.

A tingly feeling started moving up Kalissa's spine as she saw the fake bitch was still only a few feet away from their table, throwing glances at them.

"I'm going to the restroom." She grabbed her clutch purse from the table.

"Don't make me come looking for you." Nigel grabbed her hand.

"Nah, what you need to do is get that shit over there straight," Kalissa said, snatching her hand back, looking towards the wall.

Nigel looked at the girl who'd accosted him. He couldn't help but shrug.

Kalissa followed the handwritten signs signifying 'Emergency Exit/Restrooms' to the back of the club. Thankfully, there wasn't a line. It took three tries to find a halfway decent stall. The first one had pee and bloodstains on the seat: in the second one, somebody had taken a shit and hadn't flushed. The third was decent but smelled like piss.

Halfway squatting and half standing over the toilet, and still mad about that disrespectful bitch, Kalissa positioned herself so that her pee wouldn't hit the floor. After wiping, she remembered she had half a joint in her purse. It took three deep pulls before she felt the tingling sensation go away. Satisfied, she walked out, washed her hands, feeling good.

The club's mirror wasn't very clean; she had to move her head from side to side looking for a clear spot. She ran her hands through her hair, freshened up her lip gloss before smacking her lips together.

"Yep, you got it bitch." She smiled at her reflection.

Her phone rang as soon as she pushed the door open. Fumbling around for it, as soon as she hit the green button to answer, she was slammed against the wall.

"So, you thought you was going play me, bitch?"

"What?" Kalissa was so surprised she didn't know what to say as she looked into the angry brown eyes of her assailant.

Her abuser led her to the exit, roughly pulling her arm. She tried to resist being shoved like a cow to a slaughter house, but lost one of her shoes, scraping the top of her foot as he dragged her outside.

"Let go of me!" she managed to yell, before he grabbed her around the neck and slung her against the building.

"You must have thought I was a fuckboy, huh? That's what you thought?"

His spittle slapped her face as she clawed at his hands, trying to break free. She felt the blood rushing to her head and tears swam in her eyes. Thoughts of her beautiful daughter flashed through her mind as his grip tightened more and more.

The next thing she knew she was on her knees gasping for air. Nigel appeared in a flash, dragged her assailant off her, and landed an uppercut to his jaw. Her attacker roared as he bum-rushed Nigel and slammed him into the dumpster, then delivered a hook to his side and a cross to his cheek. Gagging and coughing, Kalissa rose, trying to help, but heard the screech of tires.

Pop! Pop!

Rod shot through his open window and one bullet hit the guy in his shoulder.

"Oww!" the dude howled as he went down.

With her big toe throbbing, the rest of her foot burning, Kalissa hobbled over to Nigel to make sure he was alright as Rod got out of the car.

"Lissa, help me," her attacker croaked, with his hand stretched out.

Not sure how to react, she looked at Nigel and Rod.

"Okay, I'll call . . ."

Pop! Pop! Pop!

Kalissa's eyes bulged as Rod put three bullets in her attacker's chest. Standing stock-still, she couldn't move. The man's breath turned ragged before his eyes seemingly fixed on her.

"Come on! We gotta go!" Nigel yelled, pushing her to the car.

Kalissa snatched her arm away. She clapped her hand over her mouth, hypnotized by the blackish blood seeping from under the guy. The blackness of the blood, as it trickled across the ground,

12

made her feel the bullets must have wrecked untold internal havoc on the guy's system. Nigel yelled at her. She backed away, her eyes still glued to the blood. The building scraped her back as she bumped into it. Still in shock, she managed to retrieve her shoe, then hopping painfully, she made it to the car and they peeled out of the parking lot.

C.D. Blue

For the Love of a Boss

CHAPTER 1

2005

Terry pushed Kalissa's knees up to her chest, while he pounded in her pussy. It didn't feel that great, so Kalissa grunted more out of discomfort than pleasure. That sound spurred him on, and he really went at it then.

"You love this dick, don't you?" he grunted while sweat dripped off him.

Did she? She grunted instead of answering, mainly because with her knees damn near on her shoulders, speaking was pretty much impossible.

After a few more hard thrusts, she managed to get one leg down and felt like she could breathe. Usually she enjoyed sex with him, but this encounter was a departure from the norm, and he did nothing to put her in the mood. He went harder at it, while she rolled her eyes over his shoulder.

He moaned. "Shit! Here I come, ughh!"

"Thank goodness," she murmured. He was breathing so hard he didn't even hear her.

On wobbly legs she rose and went to the bathroom. After she brought him a towel to wipe up, she cuddled next to him as he leaned back on the headboard. She noticed him staring at the ceiling. A deep sigh escaped from his mouth.

"Are you okay? Something bothering you? Kalissa asked.

Terry sighed again. "Um . . . I don't know how to put *it* to you . . ."

"What's *it*?"

"I . . . er . . . I think we need some space for a little while," Terry said.

What the fuck? He better be talking about the space his wide ass just made between her legs. She went from knock-kneed to bow-legged in a matter of minutes.

"What kind of space do you mean?" she asked, though deep down she knew exactly what he was talking about. It also hit her

15

that this had been on his mind the entire time he was sexing her. The dirty bastard didn't have the decency to talk before.

"I'm moving in with my sister," he said plainly as if talking about the weather.

Each word hit her in the stomach; she blinked rapidly to keep the tears from forming. Terry had been her dream since she was twelve years old. Unbeknownst to him, she had a mad crush on him when he was in junior high school. She used to go with her sister to the basketball games, just out of delight in watching him play. Every time she saw him, her heart fluttered: he was so cute.

When she got to high school he wasn't supposed to be there. But since he hadn't completed all his classes, he was. Having grown into almost adulthood, he wasn't as cute to her as he'd once been, but she dated him to fulfill a childhood fantasy. Here they were, seven years and one child later. The last five years he alternated between her and his first girlfriend, La'Miracle, who had just become his third baby momma.

This time was supposed to be different! Kalissa's head shook from side to side unconsciously because she couldn't believe this was happening to her. They had made future plans; he had included her in all aspects of his life this time—his friends, family, and even in his finances. The moments they had lain in bed as a family crossed her mind—him, her and their two-year-old daughter, Jamila, who adored the ground he walked on. How was she going to explain to Jamila that Mommy couldn't keep her dad at home?

Her breath got caught in her throat, making it harder to deny her tears. Determined not to hyperventilate, as she often did when she was upset, she closed her eyes and took several deep breaths.

He tenderly touched her arm, but she shot off the bed, almost falling, as the wrinkled sheets got caught around her foot.

"Did you hear what I said? I'm not breaking up with you." He kept his voice low.

Terry had done this many times in the past to a point where she should have been used to it. But this time he promised that things would be different. Her inner instinct wanted her to stomp

16

For the Love of a Boss

her feet, cry, throw and break a few things. Considering crying always broke him down, that's what she usually did. Not this time! She wasn't giving in to her inner madness, nor the way she knew would make him feel bad.

Not wanting to comprehend what he said, she tried to piece together why he wanted to leave. They had been living together in her Section Eight apartment for the last six months. She thought this time was the real thing, especially when he had proposed to her two months ago. Sure, she had a few minor meltdowns, but she had cooked, cleaned, taken care of their daughter, worked, and even dealt with his bitchy ass sisters! Now he wanted to leave.

No matter what else he said, all she heard was that he was leaving and they would no longer be together every day. Almost in a daze, she asked him calmly, "Okay, when are you leaving?"

Terry's forehead wrinkled as he raised his eyebrows and sat up straight. "I don't mean right now, maybe within the next week or two."

How could he be so calm and cruel? Not only was he leaving, he planned it for a predetermined time in the future. The timing was probably based on when his baby momma would be able to have sex. The more she thought about it, she realized everything had been great until that bitch came to tell him she was pregnant.

"We're going to be fine. I just think we were too fast with moving in together." Terry spoke quickly.

A blank stare was all she managed before she went to the bathroom to take a shower. As the water beat across her back, she looked through the clouds of steam for answers. The only answer she came up with was that shapeless, ugly ass bitch that had the nerve to give him his first son. Right before she had the baby, La'Miracle had come to Kalissa's apartment, crying.

Thinking back on that night, she realized that she should have put her foot down and told that thirsty bitch to leave. Instead, she tried to be mature and let him go outside to talk to her. It boosted her ego when he came back in, and she felt no pity when La'Miracle spent half the night walking the sidewalk in front of her apartment. Kalissa also didn't lose any sleep from the letter

La'Miracle left on her door, begging Terry to come back to her. Shit! In her mind that meant she was winning!

Somehow, some months between that night and now, she had gotten to him, probably one of the nights he claimed he had to go back to work. A cold draft of air interrupted her thoughts as she tried putting all the pieces of the puzzle together.

"Hey, listen, we are not breaking up. We can still see each other, and I'll still be here most of the time." He spoke softly after he slid the shower curtain back. His toffee-colored face appeared through the cloud of steam. With his deep-set eyes, hook nose, and thin mustache over sexy dark lips, he was the picture of contriteness. He was too thick to be considered fine, but to her he was the finest man she knew.

Since she had figured out what brought on this "space" and "moving too fast", anger quickly replaced her sadness. She snatched the water off, and stood there dripping wet, glaring at him.

"What you are *not* going to do is spend the next week or two telling me how it's going to work! If you need space, then just leave, there's no need for you to draw it out."

"I don't know why you are mad, nothing's changed." He gave her a look of annoyance.

Her inner crazy that shifted from anger to depression at the flip of a switch oozed out. Most times she was able to hide it behind a mask, but since he lived there and was still trying to play her, she lost the battle. With flaring nostrils and narrowed eyes, she let him have it all.

"You don't know why I'm mad? You said we weren't doing this again and that you were ready to settle down with me! Let's not pretend that your space has nothing to do with your new baby and baby mama. If you walk away from me and our daughter, we are through!"

"Where did you get all that from? This has nothing to do with her, but since you brought her up, you are the problem. No matter what happens, you always bring up La'Miracle. I'm tired of dealing with your jealousy when it comes to her." Terry shrugged and walked to the bedroom.

All Kalissa heard was, she was the problem and that he was tired of her. Her anger morphed into sadness, tiny pricks of feeling unwanted clouded her vision. Terry got in the bed as if it were any other night. Since he was tired of her, and her heart was filled with sadness, she knew he didn't want to deal with her tears. Grabbing her pajamas out of the drawer, she went to Jamila's room. She was in the crib, but there was also a twin-size bed in the room. Since Kalissa was only five foot one, and one hundred ten pounds, the smaller bed was fine.

Maybe she was the problem instead of La'Miracle. The tears finally came, she was tired of being abandoned, no matter how hard she tried to do everything right. It seemed as if each time she loved someone deeply, they left. In her mind there was a deficit in her DNA; she was unlovable. She knew that since childhood. Being the youngest of four, she adored and was doted on by her mother. As much as she loved her mother, it didn't stop the uncaring woman from walking out on her.

When she was ten, her mother, Maggie, left Kalissa and her two older siblings with their dad. The oldest sibling, Jennifer, was already out of the house. One morning Maggie waltzed into the room with a shabby suitcase and told them she was leaving. Life after that was never the same.

Even at a young age she hadn't been emotional, but she learned how to hide her feelings even better after her mom left. As long as she pretended not to be heartbroken and devastated, it was easier to keep up the façade of being normal. Her friends at school never knew her life had changed drastically and she shied away from meeting new friends, so that she wouldn't have to explain.#

No one on the outside of their household walls knew the extent of the damage. Their family had been torn apart. Her dad didn't know what to do. Her older sister, Mahali, acted as if nothing out of the ordinary had happened, while her brother, Khalil, became angry and distant. Kalissa, on her part, just couldn't understand why they couldn't go with her. Many parents of her school friends were divorced, but these friends of hers all lived with their mothers.

She held onto the illusion of being normal outside of the house. But after a few years, her childhood was lost. By this time her dad's mother had moved in with them. Grammy normalized things somewhat, but Kalissa was already on a track to out-of-control. She just knew how to hide it from her grandmother, or so she thought. Thinking back on it, her grandmother must have had an idea, because she began giving tutorials to show Kalissa how to use two assets: her looks and her brain.

Mahali moved to Georgia to attend college, and came back three years later. Instead of a degree, she came back with a baby, which she immediately left with their mom. Khalil joined the military, rarely came home and when he did, he brought an intense anger and attitude with him. Kalissa, whose IQ was in the gifted range at the age of nine, kept her grades up even after being introduced to weed and boys.

Once boys noticed her, she felt powerful because they were putty in her hands. Then she met Terry and he introduced her to weed. At first, she smoked it to have a connection with him, then she realized how much she liked it. Weed kept her calm. As for any hurt that came her way, a blunt soothed the pain. The pain of being dropped by him every five or six months.

Terry had been her first real boyfriend, and even though she was only fifteen, he wasn't the one who popped her cherry. But he was the first one she was able` to go out on a real date with. After their second year, things changed. He formed the habit of breaking up with her and going back to his first girlfriend, who was older, had a job, and her own car, which she let him drive.

As soon as Kalissa adjusted to being without him and met someone else, he dragged his ass back in her life. And she let him in. Only to be left again and again. Here they were, five years later, doing the same thing. Taking a deep breath to staunch the flow of tears that soaked her baby's pillow, a sliver as cold as ice shot through her heart.

20

For the Love of a Boss

Fuck love and its heartache. She vowed never to get messed up in the name of love again.

She awakened to Jamila's cries for food. Once she squared her away, she called in sick. Her life was falling apart. Who could work under those conditions?

She spent most of the day hoping Terry would change his mind. She further made sure everything, including herself, was perfect. An extra incentive for him to rethink his decisions. Her heart broke as he swooped in after work, looked at her sadly and packed his things. Jamila followed his every step and seemed confused when he hugged her and kissed her goodbye. Kalissa wanted to ask him to stay, but the words stuck in her throat when he kissed her forehead and walked out the door.

The rest of the evening was horrible. Staying busy with Jamila kept her pain at a minimum, but it spiked each time her precious daughter asked about him.

"When is Daddy coming back?" Jamila's tiny voice matched the inquiry in her eyes.

"He's not coming back to stay, but he will be back to see you sweetie." Kalissa steadied the lie in her voice.

Jamila only asked three different variations of the same question seven more times before she went to bed. As much as her feelings hurt, the grief she heard from her daughter almost killed her. She knew from Terry's first baby momma that he would be a ghost in Jamila's life.

She went from a woman with a future husband and family life, to a single mom in a matter of minutes. When she looked at her beautiful sleeping daughter, she knew changes had to be made. If she wanted to let Terry bounce in and out of her life, that was one thing. But she would be damned if she would allow him do it to their daughter. Her child had brought her more happiness in two years than any one person ever had in her entire twenty-two years. She owed her a better life.

Her positive, strong outlook crumbled when she realized her part time job wouldn't allow her a freedom from Terry. Thank goodness, she hadn't declined her child support when he asked her to marry her, but even with that she would be short.

"Damn!" She needed a plan of action, so she reached for her phone to call the one person who always had ideas. Her best friend—Taj.

CHAPTER 2

Taj dimmed the lights before he went to the kitchen to get some wine. Zandra, his girlfriend, settled on the couch with a half-smile on her face.

"I still can't believe finally I get to spend one night with you," she said in a joking tone.

"If you like the nice things I get you, then you ought to understand," Taj replied.

Zandra had been on his back for the past two weeks about taking her out and spending some time with her. He worked all day at a regular job and made his real money at night, so his time was limited. She never complained when he paid her car note, gave her money for her hair, nails and clothes.

"Oh, I like them, but I like spending time with you too. Not just the quickies when you drop off money. That makes me feel like the side chick."

Those words of hers stopped Taj in his tracks. Zandra always managed to ruin a good night with her insecurities. As far as she knew, he worked two legitimate jobs, which meant he didn't have time to wine and dine her.

"Okay, I can quit my night job, we can eat Ramen noodles and you can do your own hair. We won't be going to many places anyway." His phone rang as soon as he handed her the glass of wine, cutting off whatever smart remark she was about to make.

He listened intently while Zandra glared at him. She crossed her arms when he hung up. He knew that some shit was coming, because her whole appearance had changed. Zandra wasn't big, but her face was round and her eyes were close-set and at the moment glaring at him.

"Who was that? Your night-time boss?" She sneered.

"Nah, it was Lissa. Come on, we've got to go. We'll spend another night together." He grabbed his keys off the hook.

"Wait one damn minute! We are leaving because Kalissa called? You must be out of your fucking mind if you think I'm going somewhere. That selfish bitch may run you, but she ain't running me. Whatever she needs can wait for your next free moment." Zandra's voice had risen and she bucked her eyes.

"If you don't get your ass off that couch and come on here . . ." He trailed off and looked askance at her. "Lissa don't run me, neither do you. I said let's go."

It was either his tone or the look in his eyes, but after a short pause she got up.

"That simple bitch is going to have your ass single, sooner rather than later." Zandra tossed her purse over her shoulder as she walked out.

After he listened to her bitch and moan all the way to her house, Zandra gave him her cheek when he walked her to the door. Taj just laughed and patted her ass. As soon as he got in his car, he turned up "Candy Shop" by 50 Cent. Lissa didn't tell him what was going on, but he could tell by her voice that she was upset.

Zandra was right that he was always there for Kalissa, because she had done—and would do—the same for him. Which was more than he could say about Zandra.

He and Kalissa had been friends since they were twelve. He watched her grow from a shy pretty teenager into a beautiful woman, who still didn't realize the depths of her beauty. He kicked himself many days for being in the forever friend zone.

When she opened the door, he could tell immediately that she had been crying. Even with red rimmed eyes, hair in a ponytail, and baggy shorts with a tee shirt, she still looked finer than most women he knew

"What's up, Lissa?" Taj asked.

"Hey, Tee, sorry for bothering you, but I was about to drive myself crazy sitting here alone." She looked around at the walls.

"Where's Terry?" Taj got along fine with Lissa's boyfriend, although deep down he didn't care much for him.

"He's gone." She said it simply, but he heard the catch in her voice.

"You mean *gone*, gone? As in, moved out?" Taj sat down beside her.

Tears welled in her eyes as she nodded.

"Damn, what that chubby fucker do now?" Taj hated to see her upset, but truth be told, she deserved much better than that asshole anyway.

"He needed *space*," she said as her voice broke.

She went into the back and returned with a roll of toilet tissue. He remembered how her face looked when she told him and their other close friend from middle school, Felicia, that they were getting married. She was so happy, which rarely happened, and he thought that nigga had finally realized what he had.

"Don't worry, y'all will get back together pretty soon," Taj said softly.

"Nope, not this time! I'm done with his ass and this love shit. It is not for me." She damn near yelled.

"You didn't ever really love that nigga anyway." Taj laughed.

"What the hell are you saying? With all the shit I did for him? I did things I don't normally do; I cried about him, played his game with him, I even stole for him. Yeah, I loved him, he just didn't love me."

She spoke the truth. He remembered many times he'd fussed at her about letting that nigga run between her and the other woman. He also got onto her about clipping the register at work to give Terry gas and weed money. Thankfully, she stopped that without ever getting caught.

"You were in love with the thought of love, that's all." He watched the range of emotions that ran across her face.

"No, but for some reason, niggas think I'm a game piece. Since love has never loved me I won't fall for anybody else. These niggas want to do right when you do them wrong. If you start feeling them, then they are just like a two-liter soda, they go flat quick. Fuck it, I'ma give them just what they ask for from now on." She took the last swig of her beer. "You want a beer?"

He wasn't even sure if she saw him nod, because she made it to the kitchen so fast. She came back with two beers. He wondered how many she had already drunk, because as little as she was, she could put some beer down. She plopped down damn near in his lap when she came back.

"Anyway, what were you doing when I called?" Her breath tickled his arm, that's how close she was.

After he told her, she laughed. "So, I saved you. You should have brought me a six pack for that."

Zandra and Lissa used to be best friends. Felicia was Taj's next door neighbor growing up; he had introduced her to Lissa, then Felicia introduced Zandra to Kalissa in the eighth grade. At that time, Taj was hanging more with the fellas, and only saw them in their shared classes. The two girls hit it off immediately; if anyone saw one, the other one wasn't too far behind. After Kalissa got pregnant, things changed. Zandra began acting stand-offish and weird. Kalissa frowned anytime Zandra's name was mentioned. This just happened to be the time that Taj noticed that Zan was cute, so he knew their break couldn't be attributed to any jealousy about him. Neither woman would speak on it; Felicia didn't know what happened, so he just left it alone.

"Zandra's not that bad and you know it. Hell, she was your closest friend before I started messing with her." He looked squarely at her.

"Operative word, 'was'. If I dropped her, I don't know why the hell you picked her up. Other than you know that she's too dumb to catch on to what you do." She swallowed her beer and looked at him innocently.

The effect of her closeness and looking in her eyes made him uncomfortable as hell. Her eyes were one of her most prominent features, not only because they were deep-set, but there were flecks of green in them. A weird combination, but once she looked at a person it was hard to turn away. If their friendship didn't mean so much to him, he would be her man, and Terry wouldn't stand a chance. He would make sure she never thought about another man, but he knew that she would never go for it. She knew everything about him and he knew more than most people about her.

"I'm just playing Tee, low-key hating because you have Zandra, Felicia has a man, and as usual I have no one. Don't pay me any attention, I'm happy for you." She sounded serious, but her expression wasn't. "But you know that Zan is dumb as a box of rocks."

They laughed, but he felt bad for her when she turned to him with a sad expression.

"Taj, what's wrong with me? I can't seem to get this relationship thing right. I mean, why am I never enough for Terry?"

She didn't cry, but the look on her face—combined with her question—filled him with a strong desire for her, which overwhelmed him so suddenly he could hardly believe it. This urge made him wish Terry would just meet his death ASAP.

"It's not you, that nigga is just full of games, that's all." Taj pulled her close to him.

Most people thought Kalissa was cold and emotionless, he was one of the few people she let see the real her. He knew that she could be cold and unfeeling, but if she cared, she cared deeply. Rubbing her back seem to ebb the tension out of her, but increased his. He moved around and tried to adjust his hardening dick without being noticed.

Her hurt along with the beer made her talk and cry freely. He listened to her until she finally fell asleep; he leaned his head back and tried to doze. When he woke up, his left arm was numb because Kalissa was cuddled against him, asleep, but his manhood was wide awake and at attention. His body begged him to tell her how he felt, but his mind nixed the idea. Since he needed to check on his money, he nudged her after he rearranged himself in his pants.

"You leaving, Tee?" She rubbed her eyes as she sat up.

He stood. "Yeah, you know I need to check on these fools. I can come back, tho'," he said quietly, as he watched her stretch.

"No, that's okay. I need to do some things. But you can come back later if you have any leftovers. I need something a little stronger than beer." She grinned.

He nodded before he turned to leave.

"Taj!" she called his name loudly.

When he turned around, she met him with a kiss that landed closer to his mouth than his cheek.

"Thanks for coming. I don't know what I'd do without you." She looked up at him with a smile, but her eyes remained so sad.

Before he thought about it, he grabbed her in a hug and held her close. He lowered his face in her hair and inhaled the fruity smell while it tickled his nose. She held onto him briefly before she wiggled away.

"Ahhh, you are squeezing the life out of me," she said jokingly.

"I'll be back later, so don't do anything you'll regret" Taj admonished her because he knew how her anger got the best of her sometimes.

He glanced back at her apartment when he got to his car; she still stood in the doorway, looking lost.

The ride to the other projects took him longer because he needed to get his mind off Lissa. He had to be a different type of man when he dealt with his money. Taj worked at a warehouse during the day and sold weed and pills on the side. It started innocently enough, his uncle was the connect for the city and let him take some to school to smoke with his friends. Taj didn't share it; he sold it. Once his uncle found out, he gave him more to sell.

Taj didn't need to sell weed, but he enjoyed the extra money. He was considered one of the preppy kids at school, because he dressed nice and drove a decent car. By the time he graduated from high school, he had regular customers, added pills to his résumé, and his uncle gave him the run of one of the projects. He brought on his cousin Lorenzo, who needed the money badly. Lorenzo was his first cousin on his dad's side. They grew up close almost like brothers. Zo—as the cousin was fondly called— had moved in with his family during middle school because his mom was messed up on drugs. Well, she had been strung-out, but when she went to prison for armed robbery, they took him in.

A year after graduation, his uncle gave him the weed business because he had expanded to crack. Taj managed the pill sales himself and let Lorenzo oversee the projects. He made five times more in drug money than he did from his job, and it was growing.

His phone rang a few minutes into his ride; it was Zandra.

"Why haven't you been answering your phone?" she screamed.

"I didn't hear it," he answered calmly. He wasn't lying, because he had his phone on 'silent'.

"And I guess you didn't see that I called you? I'm tired of your shit, Taj, sick and damn tired. You left me to go to that skinny ass bitch and then you never answer your phone? But I'm supposed to believe that y'all just friends?" She sobbed.

"Lissa was having a hard time 'cuz Terry left her again. Friends go see about their friends when there is a crisis."

"Hell, then we will never get to spend time together, because Terry is always leaving her ass. She ought to stop being so bitchy all the time."

"Hey, I'm stopping at Zo's. I'll swing by when I leave," he told her, because he wasn't going to keep going back and forth with her.

"Humph, I might be here and then again I might not."

"Girl, stop playing. Your ass better be there when I get there. In fact, be naked and ready for me." He hung up before she answered because he knew that she would do just what he said.

He pulled up to the spot and before he got out, Lorenzo was walking towards him. He needed to talk to his cousin, because he looked scruffy and dirty. No matter how many times he told Zo that he was his lieutenant and not a worker, he wanted to be out there with the niggas.

"What up?" Taj greeted Lorenzo with a fist bump. He was glad too, because Lorenzo's fingernails were dirty as hell.

"Mane, we have a problem! Lil' Red in there is short on money and dope. I told him that you were on your way." Lorenzo huffed.

Taj's eyebrow shot up as he gave Zo the side eye. "What you mean, short? How short?"

Aggravation crawled up Taj's spine because he kept telling Lorenzo to manage the niggas working so that shit like this wouldn't happen. Instead he was so busy trying to sell and get some pussy that he didn't manage their set worth a shit.

Lorenzo looked at the ground before he answered. "About four or five hundred. But you know he's one of the youngins."

"Cuz, what the fuck you mean four or five hundred? That ain't fucking short, that's his whole fucking night! Why the hell can't you manage these muthafuckas?" Taj yelled.

"Don't try to put this shit on me! If I wasn't managing them, I wouldn't know how short the nigga was. Shit, you want me to do all the damn the work and all you do is, complain." Lorenzo spat.

"Nigga, shut the fuck up! Let's go see what's going on wit' this lil' nigga." Taj grabbed his .45 from under his seat and followed Lorenzo into the apartment.

Lil' Red sat on the stained sofa with an insolent look on his face. An older version of him stood beside the sofa, looking down. Taj recognized him when he walked in; this was the little dude who talked mad trash. He hadn't wanted to take him on, but Lorenzo vouched for him.

Taj looked around, the apartment belonged to one of the women Lorenzo messed around with, but she was nowhere in sight. Her absence made him feel Lorenzo must have asked her to stay behind the scenes in order to avoid undue attention.

"What up lil' man?" Taj spoke softly as he squatted in front of him.

"Nuthin', but like I told Zo, I ain't missing no money." Lil' Red looked him in his face.

The heat started in his toes and rose to his chest. This little dude took him for a fool. Not only was he lying, but he had massive attitude to go with it. Most people thought since Taj was soft-spoken, dressed conservatively and rarely gave public displays of anger, that he was soft.

Taj inhaled deeply. "Awright, since you ain't missing no money, where's the weed?"

"Just like I told Zo, I don't . . ." Lil' Red didn't get to finish, because Taj bust him in his mouth.

"Shit, man!" Lil' Red hollered as blood spurted from his lip.

"Where's my weed?" Taj asked again.

"I said I don't . . ." The next blow connected with his eye.

"That's your last lie. Do I need to ask you again?" Taj never raised his voice, but he stood and moved his hand to the back of his pants.

Lil' Red's brother pulled him up and whispered furiously in his ear. With his eye closing and his mouth bleeding, he pulled his baggy pants down. Money was taped and pinned to the inside. While he snatched it, out his brother tried to explain.

"Our mom said our lights was about to be turned off, Red was just trying to take some extra home for her."

"All you had to do was ask, nephew," Lorenzo piped up.

Now Lil' Red was shrugging and looking like the kid he was. He handed the money to Taj, holding his head down.

"Well, look like y'all little niggas going to be in the dark. Get the fuck outta here and don't come back around." Taj stepped to the right without looking up from his count.

"W-w-whatabout the money I made tonight?" Lil' Red asked at the door.

Taj frowned, "What money? I told you in the beginning what was expected of you. Take the air outside as your payment."

The two young men looked at each other and hurried out. Lorenzo fell heavily on the sofa with his legs splayed in front of him.

"Man, that was cold. You could've helped them out with their lights." Lorenzo snorted snot back into his nose.

"Did you see the way that lil' nigga lied? His grimy ass need to be in the dark for a little while. Trying to fuck me." Taj shook his head.

"Yeah, you right. What you about to get into?" Zo rubbed his dirty hands across the arms of the sofa and rolled his eyes.

Taj ignored the question. "I know you don't have enough product for today. Follow me to the spot, 'cuz I'll be busy later."

Taj shook his head because Zo thought he didn't see him rolling his eyes. What the hell did he need with a right-hand man that challenged his decisions? It was time to look for his cousin's replacement.

C.D. Blue

CHAPTER 3

Putting business out of his head, he went home, showered and changed before heading to Zandra's. The last thing he needed was to show up with the same clothes he'd worn the night before. He chose a pair of baggy black Diesel jeans with a baggy grey tee shirt. His retro Jordan sneakers completed his look.

Zandra came to the door in a see-through teddy, her lips set in a pout. As difficult as she could be sometimes, she knew exactly what to do.

"I thought you had changed your mind," she purred, sounding nothing like the woman from a few hours earlier.

Grabbing his hand, she led him to her bedroom, which was still decorated like a little girl's room. He understood that she still lived at home, but he wished she would change the decor. He forgot about that, though—once she smashed her big tits on him and stuck her tongue down his throat. He grabbed her thong and pulled it up tight through her ass crack, while grinding his hard dick against her.

Zandra knew what to do; she broke off the kiss and slithered down to her knees. Taj closed his eyes as she took him deep down her throat. He held onto the doorknob as she slurped on his long, thick dick as if it was the best thing she had ever tasted. One thing was for sure, he couldn't knock her head game.

After a few minutes, he grabbed her braids and guided his dick further down her throat. She gagged but at this point, he didn't care; his balls tingled as she opened her mouth wider until her lips met his pubic hair.

He stopped her because he didn't want to nut in her mouth; he wanted some pussy. Once his mind cleared, he pulled his pants up enough to get a condom out of his pocket.

Zandra shook her head. "We don't need that, bae. Remember I got on the pill last month."

He grimaced, not because he had forgotten, but he just wasn't one hundred percent sure she was really on the pill. When she slipped her teddy off and got on the bed with her knees on her chest, pussy splayed wide open, his dick solved the dilemma.

Rubbing his head against her slit, he found out she was only a little moist. He wasn't in the mood to give her head, so he spit on his tip and plunged right in. Zandra liked it hard, so he held her knees in place and rammed his hot meat in her center.

"Yesss! Taj, fuck that pussy, baby!" Zandra yelled.

With each stroke, she got wetter and louder, making him harder.

"Ohh, Taj this is your pussy, give me all your dick, yesss!"

A clatter from somewhere in the house interrupted his strokes. He had forgot to ask her if her mom was home!

"Your dick feels so good, you killing this pussy!"

He wasn't bothered by the noise because he knew her mom didn't care. Besides, her moans of pleasure sparked his ego. Most of all, the thrill of looking at his dick slide in and out made his balls tighten.'

As he felt the tingling, he let go of her knees and held onto the bed sheets. Zandra wrapped her legs around his as he skeeted inside her.

Either the bareback fuck or the head she had given him left him weak as hell. He lay on top her, trying to get his mind right.

"Taj, do you love me?" Zandra's voice was small as she ran her fingernail down his back.

Holding his head up, he kissed her lips, "You know I do."

"How come you never tell me?" Her voice was laced with unshed tears.

Taj rolled off her, frustrated that she wanted to talk about this now. Looking at the swirls on her ceiling, he tried to think of the right answer; to end this conversation.

"Because you know I do, that's why. Don't I show you?"

"How? By running every time Kalissa calls? That's supposed to show me that you love me?"

"Fuck! Why are you bringing that up?" Taj sat up angrily. "Don't I give you money, and keep you straight? What else you want me to do?"

34

"Treat me like I come first, instead of that fucked up hoe!" Zandra sat up too and grabbed her comforter to cover her bottom half.

Since he had busted his nut, he was able to see her clearly. Her lipstick was smeared across her chin and sweat illuminated the rolls around her neck.

"Mane, I don't have time for this shit. No matter what I do, your ass always complaining." Taj's southern drawl was more pronounced in his anger.

He snatched his pants up, slid in them before heading for the door.

"Where the fuck you going?"

Her words stopped him in his tracks. He turned around and walked back to the edge of the bed.

"Naw, the question is: who the fuck you think you talking to? Mess around and get your wig split."

Fear popped in her eyes, but she quickly hid it. "I wish you would try. My daddy would kill your ass. You want to put your hands on me because I called you on your shit about fucking that hoe."

Quick as a flash, he grabbed her face, scrunching her lips into a circle. "Keep playing with me and I'll show your stupid ass how much I care about your muthafuckin' pops."

He shoved her back hard as he released her face. She curled up on the bed and started bawling.

"I can't believe you put your hands on me! The only time you get mad is when I bring up Kalissa! I hate your ass!"

Damn! That nut wasn't even worth all this! Taj thought as he looked at her thrashing around on the bed, throwing pillows and shit.

"Zandra! Calm your ass down so that I can go to the bathroom and wash up!" He had to yell for her to hear.

He cracked the door and listened for any sounds. In case anyone was home, he knew that if her screams of ecstasy didn't wake them up, then her crazy rantings did. He peeped through the crack but didn't see anyone, so he slipped out.

Two steps into the hallway, a voice stopped him.

"Sounded like y'all were having fun for a few minutes."

Zandra's mom, Shelia, stood against the doorjamb of her room in a silky robe loosely tied together. She slid one hand in, playing with her breast and allowing the robe to open further.

Taj looked her over and shook his head. Her mom was fine as hell, and this wasn't the first time she had come on to him, but she was a hoe. Her dad worked two jobs, was never home, and the whole town knew that Shelia was fucking the owner of the store she worked at. To make matters worse, he was white!

She walked slowly to him and put her hand on his chest. Her robe was fully opened, showing everything she was working with, and she was working with quite a bit.

"If you ever want some bomb ass head without the drama, let me know." She licked her lips while her hand traveled down his stomach.

Even knowing that she was a white man's whore didn't stop his dick from rocking up. His eyes traveled down her body, stopping on her hairy bush that was parted down the middle. Zandra must have gotten her body shape from her dad's side of the family, because she had never been as fine as her mom. One part of his body wanted to take her up on her offer, but his good sense stopped him.

Grabbing her hand right when it grazed the head of his dick, he stopped her. "I don't think so, Mrs. Banks. What would your husband and daughter think?"

Coming close and rubbing her body against his, she whispered in his ear, "What they don't know won't hurt them."

She laughed as she moved back, allowing him access to the bathroom. Closing the door, the first thing he did was splash cold water over his face and dick. If he were a different man, he would hook up with Mrs. Banks sooner rather than later.

After washing up and making sure the coast was clear, he tipped back into the bedroom. Zandra was in the mirror looking at her face. Putting his hands on women wasn't his MO. He had seen his dad hurt his mom too much, but Zandra brought his beast out.

"Hey, I'm sorry for grabbing you like that. It won't happen again."

She eyed him suspiciously through the mirror. "You promise?"

He looked down at his feet as he stood behind her. "Yeah, but you got to stop being so jealous of Lissa. There is nothing going on and I get tired of you accusing me, that's what pisses me off."

"Baby, I'm sorry, I just want to be your everything." She poked her bottom lip out.

Her apology antics didn't move him, but in order to get out without the drama, he rubbed her shoulders.

"It's alright. Just chill sometimes. Did you know your mom was home?"

"Yeah, I think she's asleep." She rolled her eyes. "She had a late night."

"Naw, she was in the hallway. I wish you would tell me when we aren't by ourselves, you know I don't like that shit."

"As long as my daddy is not home, we're alright. That bitch is always trying to listen to me get my freak on."

Tired of the drama, from Zandra and her momma, he squinted at her but didn't say anything. He gave her two hundred dollars before he told her he had to dip.

When they walked up front, Mrs. Banks sat at the table, fully dressed, drinking a cup of coffee.

"Don't forget what I told you," she smirked into her cup.

"Ma, you don't have any business saying anything to Taj. If you're mad, you need to bring it to me," Zandra snapped.

She softened her tone as she looked at Taj, "Don't pay her any attention, she won't say anything."

She tried to kiss him in his mouth at the door, but he gave her a kiss on her head and got the hell from over there.

C.D. Blue

CHAPTER 4

3 weeks later

The first three weeks after Terry left were the hardest. Instead of finding a second job, Kalissa picked up more shifts as a server at her job. When she challenged herself and her mood was right, she made good money waiting on tables, even though she hated it. But it paid the few bills she had.

Her loneliness and desire for companionship hadn't diminished even with the extra hours and taking care of Jamila. Walking in her apartment, the emptiness and quiet nearly drove her into a deep depression. Taj saved her from many tears.

"Momma, is my daddy coming over today?" Jamila, at only age two, spoke better than some adults.

"I don't think so, baby, but your Uncle Taj is coming." Kalissa spoke over the lump in her throat.

Jamila's face lit up at the mention of her 'uncle.' Terry had gone back to his usual, which were rare calls and even rarer visits.

After feeding Jamila and giving her a bath, Kalissa sat on the outside step with half a blunt and a beer. Summer was ending, but it was still hot as hell, and there wasn't a breeze in sight. The temperature and smell outside matched her mood: hot and funky. Even without a breeze, the smell from the paper mill in Prattville floated through the air. Since Jamila was awake and in her crib, she only took three hits off the blunt before going back in.

Taj arrived shortly after she made it back in the apartment. Kalissa felt self-conscious. All of a sudden the food smells in her uniform intensified as he stood in her doorway, clean and smelling good. Her lifelong friend's good looks hadn't escaped her; she just tried not to look at him like that. Taj had a smooth milk chocolate complexion, with deep-set eyes and a full mouth. His tall, wiry frame filled her doorway. After sidestepping his hug, she let Jamila jump in his arms as she excused herself to take a shower.

For some reason she took longer getting dressed, although she only put on a pair of shorts, sans panties, and a tank top. After brushing her teeth, she washed her face and made sure her hair was straight. As an afterthought, she added a touch of eyeliner. Deep down Kalissa knew the extra preparations were in response to her friend's good looks and her hormones reacting to the masculinity that reeked from his pores. Sex wasn't the objective—that might change the dynamic of their friendship; but attention never hurt a soul.

Taj and Jamila's laughter reached the back of the apartment. He was the only man other than her dad that she trusted around her daughter. The horror stories she heard about children being abused and hurt from boyfriends made her scared to allow anyone around her baby. She would kill over hers. Taj sat on the floor, playing with some loud toy, while Jamila ran around him, shrieking; neither of them paid her any attention.

Lissa yelled from the kitchen as she fixed her friend a plate. "Taj, come get your food. Jamila, it's time for you to get ready for bed."

Once Jamila was in bed and Lissa cleaned the kitchen, she smiled as she watched Taj step outside with some loud weed. Of course, she followed him and sat one step beneath him.

"Do you need anything, Lissa?" Taj put the blunt between her lips.

"Nah, I'm good. You're always trying to give your money away."

"Only to you. But for real, you know if you need anything, I got you."

Looping her arms through his legs, she leaned back. "If I didn't consider you my brother, Zandra and the rest of your women would be history."

"Oh, yeah? How you figure that?" He raised one eyebrow.

"Because my coochie drives niggas crazy. It's like crack, one hit and your life will never be the same."

Taj hollered, "Damn, girl. I swear niggas be thinking you Miss Librarian when they see you. They have no idea you have such a nasty mouth!"

For the Love of a Boss

Looking at the time, she knew her neighbors would be coming in soon. With all her other problems, the last thing she needed was to be put out for smoking weed on the steps. They didn't seem like the type to turn her in, but she didn't trust very many people. Once inside and settled on the sofa, she looked at her friend. He wore sweats and a tee shirt. But, as with everything else he wore anytime, he looked good. His cologne was in her nose. She found his body warm and hard.

"I thought you had to work tonight?" said Lissa.

"I took some vacation time. To be honest, I'm thinking about quitting, I don't need that little change."

"Oh, okay, that would be smart. Just get a car tag that says 'dope boy', while you at it. You might not need the change, but what you really don't need is people talking and wondering. But carry on, I don't know what I'm talkin' about."

He gave her a thoughtful look, "You're right. The thing is, my money is coming so strong. I know if I direct more energy to it, I'll be set."

"Mmm, hmm you said that last year. You said you were getting out of it this year. But if you are staying in it, at least be smart about it. I thought your cousin was helping you run it?"

Taj rolled his eyes and told her about the problems he had. She didn't know what came over her, but as he sat and talked about replacing his cousin with someone stronger, he exuded power. The sofa shifted as she sat on her knees and leaned over to kiss his cheek. He turned suddenly and the next thing she knew they were tonguing each other.

His mouth tasted like peppermint. His hands were hard as they ran across her body, pulling her in his lap. The heat from his lap set her on fire. His hardness poked her and made her want to stroke, lick, and feel him inside of her. Her hand went to his hair as the tip of her tongue teased the top of his mouth. The only thing that brought her to her senses was when he slid his finger up the side of her shorts. As bad as she wanted to hump his finger, she remembered that this was the only best friend she had. If they fucked, their friendship would be ruined, that was for sure.

A groan escaped her as she dragged herself out of his lap, but not before running her hand up his thigh.

Oh, my goodness! she thought as her hand connected his hardness. His dick was down his thigh! Her eyes watered as she moved to sit beside him again. *Was their friendship that important?* she wondered before common sense prevailed.

"Sorry, I guess that loud got me feeling some kind of way." She laughed nervously.

"Was that it?" His voice was husky.

She looked from his eyes, to his sexy lips, back to his lap while trying to compose herself. "Yeah, I guess. Anyway, Tee, this idea would be worse than you quitting your job. I know all your secrets. If we go any further, you won't tell me about all the women in your life, but I'll still wonder about them. Then you'll have to deal with me being suspicious and having meltdowns. It won't work."

Her words rushed out because if she didn't get them out and watch him arrange himself one more time, they would end up in the bed.

"Yeah, I guess you're right," Taj said quietly and wiped his hand down his face. "But if your shit is like crack, you won't have to worry about other women."

"Umm, sir, seems like you have the crack pipe. But the way my life is set up right now, I don't need dick problems. Let's just leave it alone."

"For now, we will leave it alone. For now," he whispered before kissing her again.

Once more she questioned how important their friendship was and it would be an added bonus to fuck him away from Zandra. Taj meant too much to her to play him like she had done others, so she scooted away.

"Taj, stop. I can't do this, no, we can't do this. Our friendship means too much." She groaned, and her pussy cried.

Disappointment filled his eyes, but he agreed. After she went to the bathroom to slow down her wetness, she came back to the front and sat across from him in a chair. After a few uncomfortable minutes, they went back to their original conversation. Her body didn't recover that quickly; because as soon as he left, her fingers were in her shorts. As her body shook and shivered, she imagined her best friend shooting a hot load of come inside her.

***

A few days later she drove to meet Taj and Felicia for lunch. She used working extra hours as her excuse to not spend as much time with Taj. He knew her so well she was sure he could tell she was avoiding him. She felt he should understand. If she explained how often she masturbated thinking about him, he would understand better, but hell would freeze over before she did that.

She squeezed her hooptie in between Taj's Dodge Charger and a Lexus, then pulled her mirror down to make sure her face was straight.

Taj was at a table and raised his hand when she walked in. She caught the eye of one cutie as he sat at the table with a woman. He smiled and gave her a nod.

"Stop flirting and bring your ass on." Taj laughed.

"It's hard out here for a pimp, but you know that." She laughed as she gave him a hug. She was glad that their friendship hadn't suffered from their 'one night'.

"Shit, I didn't stop no one from eating when I walked in, like you did. Every nigga in here had slob coming out their mouth. But that one you was flirting with is going to get his eyes dotted if he keep mean mugging me." Taj leaned back.

"They may be looking, but the thing is, the only ones that approach me have one eye, arm, or leg. And if they are cute, they don't have a job and have fifty-'leven kids that they don't take care of. Now I see why I kept running back to Terry: it's hard out here." Her favorite soda was right in front of her; she sipped it as she looked at her best friend, and he was looking good.

Taj wore white jeans, with a navy-blue golf Polo shirt and matching canvas shoes. A fresh line up, shave and his sexy lips completed the package. Her hormones were in overdrive about her best friend.

"It ain't that hard. Cet asked about you. He's a good guy." Taj winked before he looked down.

"Who is Cet? 'Cuz I know you are not talking about Cedric who is the same height as me? No, thanks. It would be nothing but bad luck if I fall in love and then proceed to have a bunch of midgets. Where did you see him?" She wanted to change the subject because Cedric was not her type.

"I'm putting him in Lorenzo's spot, 'cuz Zo is so busy chasing pussy he keeps messing up." Taj's expression became serious.

Kalissa's attention was caught by the cutie she saw earlier as he walked out of the bathroom and passed their table. "Hmm, of course he's chasing it, because pussy will never chase him."

The entrance of Felicia interrupted them. Kalissa just smiled. Her friend was tall, big, beautiful and flashy

"Scoot over, Taj, I need to look at this heifer! Girl, I thought you was heartbroken? Heartbroken folks don't look like this!" Felicia sat down next to Taj.

Kalissa smirked, "You're late! I'm over that mess."

"Damn, that was quick!"

"It's too many niggas out here to spend too much time crying about one."

"Well I'm glad because I saw him out with La'Miracle the other day," Felicia murmured while looking into her cup.

"That's not surprising, I knew that's where he would he end up. She can keep him this time."

Taj cleared his throat, "He wasn't ever good enough for you anyway. The right one will come along."

"I hope it's not anytime soon, I'm about to give all these niggas just what they been asking for," Lissa smiled at the server as he approached the table.

After they ordered, Felicia laughed "Now what were you saying? You going to give who, what?"

"She was just talking, Felicia, you don't have to report everything you see. Damn!" Taj scowled.

"I was just—"

"It's alright, Fefe, I truly don't care. I have realized that men like to play games, don't want nobody to truly be for them, and they gonna get just that from me. Women have spent centuries being abused by men, played by men, having to diminish our shine for their egos, and for what? For current men to be too lackadaisical to take care of us and their children."

Both of her friends looked at her as if she was crazy. Taj broke the spell.

"Damn, sometimes I forget how smart you are, but you're wrong on this one. There are plenty of good men out here. I know I'm one of them."

With a quick roll of her eyes she responded, "I'll keep my opinion on that to myself since you are the best friend I could ever ask for."

It didn't escape her that Taj watched her lips as she sucked through her straw.

"You gonna run off some good men with that attitude."

"That's exactly what I'm talking about! All our lives, and I'm sure Fefe will agree, we're told not to do this because boys won't like you. Don't be this or that if you want to find a good man. Why I got to find him? His ass should be looking for me because I'm the one who's going to hold it down and make things right at home. Why do we women have to act like a nigga is coming out of a Cracker Jack box? That's why they walk around acting like they have all the choices and we just need to conform to what they want. Get the fuck out of here with that."

Fefe nodded while Taj cut his eyes at her. Before either could speak, their food came. Taj and Lissa had burgers and fries, while Felicia got a steak, baked potato and some broccoli. There wasn't anything wrong with her thyroid, she just liked to eat.

"All I'm saying is that you shouldn't judge all men by a select bad few. What if you run across a good one and do him wrong?"

Chewing her food slowly while Taj looked at her, she shrugged. "That's just a chance I'll have to take. If I don't let them get too close I won't know that they're good anyway. All of them are good until they get you where they want you."

45

"No, it's the kind of man you choose. Look at Cet, he's a good man and you won't give him a chance."

"Wait a minute, Taj! I know you ain't talking about Lil' Cet. He is too little, I mean he would have to raise his arms over his head just to get them around my waist." Felicia laughed at her own joke.

"Just what I'm talking about! Y'all women be so focused on the physical look, and then wonder why you can't find a good man."

"Looks aren't the only thing, but damn when he has to run to keep up when you walking, it plays a part," Felicia winked at Lissa.

"Hmm-mmm, Cet ain't no good either. Remember those two girls fighting over him at school? And come to think of it, neither one of them was the baby momma that turned up a few months after that. No, thank you."

"When Cet comes up, and he is coming up soon, don't be asking me about him."

Lissa rolled her eyes. "Wait, he's on the come up? I think I can find a place for him in my purse."

As hard as he tried not to, even Taj burst out laughing.

"Who the hell is that? Humph, it shole isn't his baby mama." Fefe abruptly stopped laughing as she looked over Kalissa's shoulder.

After a quick glance over her shoulder, she was surprised to see it was the cutie from earlier.

"Girl, you know him? Where do you know him from?"

"He's, like, my second or third cousin. He hangs out with my brothers," she said while smacking her lips and waving her hand dismissively.

"You never told me you had a cute cousin! You always introduced me to the trolls in your family."

Felicia came from a big family and they all seemed to live in town. Everybody was either her cousin or brother.

"I guess I was working up to him. Anyway, you said you didn't want a man right now." Felicia gave her the duck lips.

46

After a few minutes, Kalissa stole another glance behind her and was disappointed to see that the couple was no longer there. Once she finished eating, she grew bored and restless, but she had the best excuse to break away. She always picked Jamila up early on her off days, for quality time. No matter how bad she messed up with relationship and love, she loved the hell out of her daughter and received it back ten-fold.

Hugging her friends and promising to go out one night with them, she left. Sadness descended on her when she realized that she'd lost an opportunity to flirt. Her ban only included serious relationships; flirting and hooking up didn't count.

"Hey, ma . . . can I go wit' you?" A deep voice broke through her thoughts.

It was the cutie from the restaurant! Tall, slim, with a latte-colored complexion and light brown eyes.

"Not today, I've got to pick my daughter up." Although she turned him down, she stopped.

"Okay, that's cool. What's your number and maybe we can hook up some other time?" He smiled.

"Weren't you with your girlfriend in there?" The girlfriend could be a casualty of war, but she needed to know what type of man he was.

"Nah, she was just a friend." He held his phone out to her.

Alarms rang in her head, but he was too cute to turn down! After she stored her number in his phone, he kissed her hand when she handed it back to him. Electric shocks went through her; she jumped back slightly.

He looked at his phone. "Kalissa, I'm Nigel. I'll holla at you soon."

Before she pulled off, she looked back at him and thought about the electricity that flowed through her from his touch. That meant one thing: run! When it came to men, she liked to be in control of her feelings. She couldn't control them if she got electrocuted every time he touched her. Nope, nope, she was concentrating on her job and her child.

"Hell nah, Mr. Nigel, I don't need you in my life right now."

C.D. Blue

CHAPTER 5

Pulling into the parking lot of her job, she had fifteen minutes to spare. Chuckling, she pulled up her account for the fourth time. All the extra hours and work she put in paid off. For two days she worked as the relief supervisor and as a server on the other days. Her bank account showed the difference.

Tap, tap. Looking to her left it was sour-faced Brian. He was the main cook and the only guy that didn't flirt with her or even talk to her.

"Yes?" It came out breathless because he had actually scared her.

"I need you to move your car. The big folks from corporate are coming today and they don't want any employees to park in the front."

Frowning, she started her car, and Brian walked away as if the plague was coming through her window. Giving him a long look, she noticed he wasn't that bad looking.

Rotating her head from side to side to get the kinks out of her neck, she smiled. As much shit as she talked to her friends about being a pimp, she barely had a life. Between working all the time and her daughter, her free time consisted of sleeping. The few dates she had were bombs and she hadn't had sex since Terry, Mr. Big Dick himself.

It was time to live a little bit and Brian looked as if he needed to have fun too. There wasn't anything more exciting than to change a man's mind when he didn't seem to want to be bothered. Pulling her mirror down, she applied her lip gloss and ran a comb through her hair. *Perfect!* she thought.

As the day wore, on she toned down the playful, somewhat abrasive, persona she always carried at work, and every so often she would throw Brian a glance. He paid her no mind and the one time he did look her way, he frowned so hard she turned her head. What had she done to this man?

"Kalissa? Can you come to my office for a minute?" Torrey, the head manager, called.

Following his bowlegs to the back, she forgot about Brian, because Torrey was fine, older, had money and had all the women in the restaurant thirsty. One major problem kept her from setting her sights on him: he was married.

"Hey, I wanted to let you know that you have been doing a great job as relief supervisor," he started slowly.

"Thank you." That was all she could think to say.

"There is an opportunity coming soon and I want you to think about it before you give me an answer. I know that you have a child and this might not be the best thing for you."

He was staring at her, at her mouth to be specific, as he rambled on. She was shocked that he knew she had a child. It made her feel a little special because he didn't seem to talk or know much about his employees.

"Okay, what is it?'

"The night supervisor's job will be open next month and I think you will you be the perfect person. It pays more, but it's also at night. That's why I said you should think about it."

Nights were not appealing to her, but more money was definitely something she wanted. Calculating how this could work in her favor, she looked at him challengingly.

"Yeah, I'll think about it, since you know I'm a single parent, and I'm not sure if nights will work for me.

"I understand that." He looked at her as she licked her lips. "What if you only do two weekend nights and the rest of your time is days?"

Raising her eyebrows, she smiled. "That might definitely work! Let me see if I can get my babysitting situated and I'll let you know."

'Okay, I think this will work. I have big plans for you."

"Is that so?" She flirted shamelessly, standing close enough to feel the heat off his body.

"Yep, this is just the beginning. Play your cards right and you might end up the front end manager. I've had my eyes on you and I know you're smart enough for it."

He sat at the desk with his legs open, staring at her, his lust apparent. She slid in between his legs, leaned forward and whispered in his ear.

"I am smart enough and so much more," she let her bottom lip touch his earlobe.

His eyes told her that he wanted to say something, but Tammy her supervisor interrupted.

"Well, here you are, Kalissa! Your people on table fifteen are looking for you." She squinted as she eyed the two of them.

"Okay, thanks!" Kalissa stepped back and around her supervisor. Rolling her eyes, she fixed her face before she went to the table. She hated waiting on these damn folks! Some of them were okay, but some of the folks tried to act as if she was beneath them, because she was a server. The couples were the worst! If she was nice to the man, the women copped attitudes, as if they didn't realize she was trying to make some money. Another reason she needed that promotion: she hated serving.

"Hey, pretty lady. Can you help me?"

Glancing over at table 20, she saw Cedric with two other guys. Stopping her eyes from rolling, she stopped at their table.

"Hey, Cedric. This isn't my table. Sorry."

Before she could get away, he grabbed his menus, got up and flicked his head to the side to let his friends know to follow suit.

"Where's your table at? I want you."

Trying to hide her impatience, she led them to the one free booth she had open. She had to admit, Cedric kept himself up. He had on an oversized red hoodie with some black jeans and some red and black Adidas. His friends were dressed similar, but they were taller and cuter.

"Kalissa, these are my cousins, Desi and Duke. Me and Kalissa grew up together," he said to his cousins, grinning.

They spoke. Desi was a milk chocolate cutie with a brilliant smile, but somewhat chunky, while Duke was a darker, slimmer chocolate cutie with a bored look. Although they were taller than Cedric, that wasn't saying much, both men were about five feet eight inches tall.

"What y'all want to drink?"

Shortly after stepping in the kitchen area to fix their drinks, she heard a scream, dishes breaking, and everybody was running to the front. Stepping between two cooks, she looked on in horror as Cedric and some tall dude with dreads were going at it! The tall dude pushed Cedric's head back with his finger. Lissa chuckled until she saw Cedric pull out a chrome gun bigger than him! His cousins were behind him, hands in their hoodies looking as if they were ready to draw. People in the restaurant started scrambling to get out. Tammy was the first one out the door. The servers on the floor either headed to the door or back towards the kitchen, whichever they were closest to.

Torrey ran from the back, with his phone in his hand, yelling at a few of the cooks to come out with him. Nobody moved, they didn't want to get caught in the line of fire.

Kalissa knew Torrey had called the police, so she looked towards Cedric, hoping he would take his ass on. The tall dark skinned guy held his hands up and backed up with an ugly sneer across his face. Catching Cedric's eye, she rolled her eyes towards the door, hoping he caught the hint. He did. They all flew out the door, and the next thing that was heard was rubber burning the asphalt.

Torrey ran to the door while everyone else took a deep breath. Some people laughed as if they weren't scared; others collected their belongings to signify that their shift was over.

"See? This why we can't make no money . . . these niggas in Montgomery always trying to shoot up shit!" one of her co-workers whined.

Another coworker cackled. "Gurl, I know that's right. That lil' short one looked kinda like a nerd until he pulled out that stick!"

"That's what y'all like! Them hood niggas! Y'all will run them niggas down, but won't give a hardworking man like me a chance!" one of the cooks said in a grumbling tone.

"Man, ain't nobody looking at your ass 'cuz you ugly and cheap!"

Everybody laughed until Torrey came to the back looking shell-shocked. He marched over to Kalissa.

"Hey, who were those guys?"

Keeping her hand around the glass she had been holding, she cocked her head to the side with an innocent look. "I have no idea. Why are you asking me?"

"I thought I saw you talking to them." Torrey looked at her closely.

"Nope, they wanted to sit in my station, so I moved them and got their drink orders. That's all." She shrugged as she poured out the soda.

"I thought I heard one of them say your name, Kalissa?" the whining co-worker piped up.

Kalissa's head spun around, "No. You did not."

Looking back at Torrey, she saw the suspicion in his eyes, but before he could say anything else the police walked in.

Kalissa walked to the locker area, hoping her no one noticed how bad she was shaking. Her co-worker watched her distrustfully.

C.D. Blue

CHAPTER 6

The sweat dripped from his head as he sat on Cet's porch, waiting for him to finish cutting his mom's grass. Who the fuck cuts grass in the middle of the day? Then he realized that why he was here. No matter what hardship or heat in this case was faced, Cedric did what he said he was going to do.

"Alright man, what's up?" Cedric stopped the mower and wiped his face with a towel.

"Can't we go inside and talk? It's hot as hell out here." Taj wiped more sweat off his face.

"Naw, man, my mom don't like anybody in the house when she isn't home. I have to respect that."

Nodding, Taj replied, "Let's sit in my car then, I just want to holla at you for a few moments."

Taj couldn't even talk until the air started blowing cool; the heat had zapped his energy and thoughts. And he had only been in it for a few minutes, while Cedric looked unbothered after cutting the grass with a push mower!

"Look, I see you have been working hard with us and I want to make you my right hand man, my second-in-command. If you want it."

Cet's eyes widened as he raised his hand for some dap. "For real? Man, of course I want it! But what about Zo? He don't want it no more?"

Taj raised his eyebrows, "Let me handle Zo. I just want to outline what I need you do and work out your dollars."

Cedric shrugged. After going over the details, he looked at Taj strangely when he got to the part about bringing more people onboard.

"I have two cousins I wanted to bring in the game, but Zo said we didn't need them. I told him that especially since we have Mollys and powder, they have connections at State and A U M." Cet said, referencing Alabama State University and Auburn University in Montgomery. The two largest universities in town.

"Hmm, when was this?" Taj tried to keep the anger out of his voice.

"Shiid, about a month ago. I saw how the fellas were struggling. Hell, I was struggling too, trying to keep up. And I knew that the college crowd would bring us more dough." Cedric sucked in his teeth.

Nothing clarified that he had made the right decision than this conversation. He had just talked to Zo about trying to get more workers out and Cet's cousins had never been mentioned. The only person Zo had mentioned was some freak he was fucking with.

"Tell your cousins to come see me. Just set up a time, sometime this week, and we'll set them straight."

"That's what's up! I'll do that, but there is one more thing. What's Kalissa doing, I mean is she seeing anyone?"

Taj laughed and before he could answer, Cedric cut him off.

"Man, I saw her the other day and she looks better than when we were in school. That woman is so pretty and now that we are going to be bringing in the extra money, I can set her straight."

"Umm, I think Lissa is seeing someone right now, but I'll let her know you asked about her again."

"Shiid! I can't help it. With her on my arms and being your second-in-command that's all I need."

"Alright, I need to get moving. Don't forget about your cousins. What's their names anyway?"

"Desi and Duke. I promise they are straight and they are going to hook us up on that college scene."

Once Cedric got out of the car, Taj headed to Smiley Court, where he knew Zo hung out at. At first, he was going to wait a couple of days before he told him, but he was so mad with what he just found out he was going to tell him right now.

Once he crossed over the bridge on the boulevard, the scene changed. Wasn't nothing on this side but fast-food restaurants, gas stations and old hotels that had become a haven for druggies and prostitutes. No matter how much money Zo made he would never leave this side of town. Taj shook his head.

For the Love of a Boss

Zo was at the front of the projects at his baby momma's house. It was actually her momma's house, but the same thing. Taj pulled up beside Zo's dusty, old Altima. Not only would he not get a newer car, but he refused to wash the one he had. Taj knew that Zo had enough money to do better, he just didn't want to. He refused to get any type of job to justify having any type of income and he spent most of his money gambling, drinking, and buying diapers.

"What up, cuz?" Zo raised his hand for some dap, then lowered it when Taj just stared at him.

"What's up is that Cet told you about some new workers and you brushed him off. What the fuck, man? You know we need more people."

"Hold the fuck up! You coming at me about what that bitch ass Cet done told you? Nigga, we don't need his corny ass folks. All they probably gonna do is get us locked up."

"Cuz, how the hell you know they corny? Yo' ass didn't even take the time to meet 'em! Looka here, I need you to step back and evaluate what the fuck you doing. From now on, I just want you to keep an eye on the guys on the streets. You too damn busy chasing pussy and playing while I'm trying to grow."

"Get the fuck out of here! Playing? Ain't nobody playin', I get you yo' money on time and it's always right. You saying I ain't your Chief no more?" An ugly glare crossed his face. "So Cet ass trying to rat me out so that he can get my spot. That grimy muthafucka."

"Nope, it ain't like that. I'm trying to grow bigger and get more money and you trying to stay the same. First off, you wasn't never no chief, but now you just got bumped down. and Cet is my second-in-command. You heard?"

Zo looked down at the ground, but before he responded his girl Ureka came out. She did not fit her name, she looked more like *Damn!* She was big everywhere but her legs looked like chicken legs and she always wore something short to show them.

"Hey, Taj! Aieee, look at your new whip, I like that. Zo keeps telling me that he's getting me one, but he said—"

"Bitch, stop running yo' mouth and git yo' ass back in the house!" Zo drowned out whatever she was about to say.

"Boy, you better stop trying to show out. I thought you said you was taking me to the store to get my WIC?" Ureka said.

"Aight, man . . . handle your business, I'll get at you later." Taj didn't want to be involved in their drama. He knew that Zo hit on Ureka and the only thing he couldn't understand was why she stayed with him. But none of that was his business.

"Don't think we finished talking about this shit. I ain't through."

"Well, I am. Go get your babies some milk and I'll holla."

As soon as he got back in his car, Zandra called.

"Hey, baby. What you doing?"

"Leaving Ureka's with Zo, what's up?"

"She still with him? Oh! Well I guess there is someone for everyone. Are you on your way over?"

"As soon as I run by Lissa's job. She hasn't called back and I know Jamila's birthday is coming up."

He heard her take a deep breath, but she didn't say anything, which was a blessing. She had gotten better about his friendship with Kalissa, but not by much.

"Okay. Well, I'm here waiting on you."

He knew that her I'm-here-waiting statement was a backhanded way of telling him, *don't take too long.* Hanging up after promising her it wouldn't be too long, he had to admit he was more excited about seeing Lissa. They hadn't hung out in a while because he had been busy and her schedule was tight, working long hours trying to take care of business. He could only respect her grind. As for Zandra, once she found out how he got his cash and how much he had, she changed from full time work to part-time. He was still shaking his head when he pulled up in the parking lot of Applebees.

Lately, with the way women reacted to him, he knew he had come a long way from his younger days. The hostess gave him the once-over. But before she said anything, Lissa bounced up to the front.

"Look at you, all fly and shit!" she said as she hugged him.

"This your friend, Kalissa?" The skinny hostess who looked to be no more than seventeen squeaked.

"Yes, friend. But you might as well stop staring because this ain't no dating game," Lissa shot back as she led him to a table in the back.

He glanced back and saw the dislike in the girl's eyes before she turned her head.

"Uh-oh, I think she just called you a name. I see you wearing that supervisor title." Taj joked with her. He knew that she had recently been promoted to relief supervisor, Taj felt sorry for the employees working for her.

"I don't care about these bitches and hoes in here. They act like they work at a club, always trying to hook up with someone. Then when the niggas hit it and don't come back, they crying and we have lost a customer. Anyway, what brings you here? You want something to drink or eat?"

Taj was laughing too hard to answer. Her tongue could be brutal, but for him that's what made her special. People didn't realize that her book sense was just as sharp as her street sense; it just depended on the day of the week.

"Nah, I'm straight."

"So, you just came to see me?" Being a natural flirt, she didn't realize that her seductive tone and look did something to him. And she didn't need to know, so he played it off.

"Yes, since you won't answer my calls. You know I need to know what my baby wants for her birthday."

Her eyes sparkled, "You know if you weren't my best friend, I would marry you! With everything you have going on, you still remembered her birthday!"

"You know that's my girl. What does she need?" He stopped her before she spoke. "I tell you what, I'll just give you the money and you get it."

He peeled off five hundreds and handed it to her. Her eyes grew big and she squealed.

"What do you want me to get her?"

"Whatever she needs." Taj stood and smiled at her.

Lissa stood too and gave him a tight hug while she whispered in his ear, "Who would have thought that when you tried to cheat off my paper in the sixth grade, you would turn out to be the best thing that ever happened to me?"

"I did." He laughed. "I got to run, Zandra is waiting on me."

Rolling her eyes up, she frowned. "Don't bring that cow to my baby's party, just leave her grazing."

Unable to help himself, he laughed. "You need to forgive and forget.

CHAPTER 7

Taj watched Zo mean mug Cedric before he began their meeting. They were sitting in Island, a Jamaican restaurant on the west side of town. Not only was the food good but at this time of day, it was nearly empty; no one hovered around trying to get a tip. Taj knew how his cousin's temper could get, which was why he chose a public place.

"Okay, I wanted to tell both of y'all about the changes at one time. Before I start, realize that this is non-negotiable. It is what it is." He looked from one man to the other.

Zo sat back with his arms crossed, while Cedric raised his eyebrows, but kept one eye on the man to his right. The difference between them was night and day. Zo was around six feet two, with nappy dreads, a grill, and was always dressed slouchy. Cedric was five feet five, wore his hair low and was always neat, almost preppy.

"Zo, you gonna continue supervise the same crew you been handling," Taj started as Zo grinned. "But Cet is gonna be the chief, and he's going to oversee the cash flow, new areas, and get more workers."

"Yo, you really gonna do this shit? I'm yo' fam' and you putting this lil' ass nigga over me?" Zo scowled.

Taj scratched his forehead. "I told you about this, man! Ain't shit changed! You'll be doing the same thing you been doing."

"With this mini nigga looking over my shoulder? This is straight trash, just garbage!"

"Nigga, you got one mo' time to call me lil', before I show you how big my other dick is." Cedric spoke calmly and quietly.

"You think you the only one got one? Nigga, we can go out-side and I'll fill your *lil'* ass full of lead." Zo sneered at Cet.

"Man, y'all cut that shit out! We here for all of us to make money and y'all acting stupid. If things work out like I plan, we all gonna be rolling in dough. Stacks upon stacks."

Cedric's eyes lit up and raised his fist for some dap. "That's what's up. If my pockets long, I can work with anybody."

Taj turned to Zo, "You cool, cuz?"

"Just make sure my pockets fat and nobody gets the big head," he grumbled.

"Cuz, you a trip!" Cedric laughed. "I've got to run on campus and see what's popping. You got the bill? Or you need some cash?" He looked at Zo with chuckle.

"Man, take your midget ass on. My shit can't even fit in yo' little boy pockets."

Taj felt Cet flinch, so he held his arm out.

"A'ight, mane. Be safe and hit me up later," Taj said, wiping his mouth.

Zo just sat with his arms crossed. Taj glared at him after Cet left.

"Cuz, why you keep acting like that?"

"So you think I'm just supposed to be a'ight with you putting that pussy ass nigga in my spot?"

"It ain't like I kicked you out. I'm just trying to get some order in the business, that's all. You a'ight with that?"

"I guess I have to be. I just don't see what's wrong with the way we been doing things."

As they ate in silence, he thought of how to explain to his cousin his dream without giving away too much.

"Mane, do you want to be on the streets forever? When we was just doing it in school to buy clothes and shit, it was different. The bigger we get, these niggas want to steal what you have instead of coming up on their own. I'm thinking big, like, legitimate big."

"Huh? How big you think these white folks gonna let you get? Here in the Gump?"

Sometimes his cousin was so simple it aggravated the hell out of him. "If we both think like that, we might as well get a job at a fast food restaurant right now. I don't know about you, but I'm grinding until I get there. I'm not going to be a dopeboy forever."

"Then you might want to sell rock if you want to make it big," Zo said, spreading his arms.

When he was younger he wondered what not seeing the forest for the trees meant, but dealing with Zo taught him well.

"Naw, mane. I'm not going down like that. You just wait and see," he said sourly.

Leaning in close, he lowered his voice, "These college kids and white kids want pills and powder. We can let Unc' handle the crack, with the skanks and halfway dead folks, while we come up on the other end."

"So, you think you gonna go up in these white folks neighborhood selling pills and powder and not get popped? As soon as they see your black ass over there more than twice, they'll be calling the cops."

Taj sat back wishing Zo had paid a little more attention in school, because this nigga was stupid!

"Nah, we don't go to them unless it's the club or campus, they'll come to us once they see we the real deal. Think, Zo, all the rappers and everybody talking about pills and shit! Ain't nobody talking about crack but these ho ass project niggas!"

"Whatever, it's your thang, I guess," he mumbled.

Zo leaned forward, still looking pissed. "You told Unc' about Cet?"

"Nah, not yet, I didn't think I had to. Look, mane, Unc' is our connect, he don't run the business. I guess you forgot he gave it to me to run, 'cuz he didn't want to fool with weed anymore."

"Nah, nigga, he gave it to us! You just like to act like you running things." Zo's nose flared and he was breathing hard.

"Who the fuck is you talking to? If he gave it us, why he told me to run it and let you help? I'm trying to grow and you just want make enough to buy them stanking ass cheap ass hoes some shoes. Don't try me, nigga."

Zo pushed his plate forward and grabbed his straw to get something from between his teeth. Nodding, he narrowed his eyes as he and Taj had a stare down.

"Okay, Taj, I see how you really feel. It's cool. We'll do it your way for now. I see these college hoes and those stuck up bitches you like to hang around done went to your head. Just remember I'm your fam', and none of these other niggas or bitches gonna have your back like me."

"Look, cuz, you still my A-one, I don't know why you tripping. Ain't nothing changed! I got your back and I know you got mine, we gonna make this money together."

***

Chris Brown blared loud enough from her Bluetooth speaker, but not loud enough to wake Jamila up. She was off the next day and a six-pack chilled in her fridge, her phone was set on vibrate because she didn't want any interruptions. The night before being off was always reserved for her to chill alone.

Her focus was back where it needed to be: on making money and taking care of her daughter. The heartbreak she had faced from Terry was gone. Nobody in the world could recover from being broken-hearted better than her. Her only regret was Jamila not growing up in a two-parent family.

A heavy knock on her door broke her free from her memories. A look through the peephole showed Taj's cousin Lorenzo. Kalissa scrunched her nose up because she didn't care for him, but she also knew that it would be easy to get rid of him.

"Hey, what's going on?" she addressed him as she swung the door open.

"I'm looking for Taj, he said he was over here." Lorenzo tried to look past her, inside her apartment.

"He told you he was here? I haven't seen Taj since two days ago." Standing her ground in front of her door, she raised her eyebrows in confusion.

"Yeah, he text me and said he was at his girl's house." Lorenzo's finger swept over his phone.

"Ahh, well, since I'm not his girl, that explains why you are at the wrong place." Kalissa started closing her door.

"Aww, shit! I thought you and Taj was finally kicking it." Zo grinned, showing his gold teeth.

64

Tired of him and the lies he was telling, she gave him the thumbs up as she once again tried to close the door. He got a straight mean mug when he placed his foot on her door.

"Since I'm here, you wanna blaze one?" A blunt appeared in his hand.

After her break-up with Terry, she had toned down her weed smoking, but she still liked to smoke it! And free weed was the best weed!

Forcing a smile, she let him in, calculating how long it would take to get rid of him. Four hits and he would have to leave. She walked to the back, closed Jamila's door and placed a towel underneath it. Just because she smoked, her daughter needed none of it.

"I see you was getting your drink on, with your music playing and everything. You got another one?"

Damn! She hated sharing her beer with a man, and she especially hated a man that begged for one.

"Fire it up," she said as she headed to the kitchen. He needed to take his musty-looking ass on.

When she made it back, he passed her the blunt as she passed him a beer. At least he didn't hog it. When the smoke went through her, she held it in as long as she could before she coughed it out. It went straight to her head! Either it had been too long since she smoked or Zo had stepped his game up. She stiffened as she felt him pat her back.

"I'm good," she said as she took one more toke before passing it back to him.

"Lissa, girl, you look good as hell," Lorenzo said through a haze of smoke. "I don't know why Taj won't hook up with you. I thought y'all was a couple."

"Now you know damn well that Taj is with Zandra, stop acting simple."

"Well, if it was me, you would be mine. You have always been the prettiest to me."

With what she had on and how she looked, she knew that the compliment was hollow. Since she had been preparing for a night of relaxation by herself, she had on a shapeless duster and her hair was tied up. Feeling her eyes tighten, she held up her hand. "Don't get crazy, Zo. We ain't smoking angel dust and I ain't having no hallucinations."

She laughed so hard at her own joke she failed to see his expression change. Lorenzo was quiet after that and after a few more hits, she knew he had to go. Her body felt too loose and she wanted to drop off to sleep.

"Alright, Zo, it's time for you to go. I've got to go to work in the morning." The lie fell off her tongue effortlessly.

"Okay, can I use your bathroom, first?" There was some kind of look in his eyes, but she didn't spend much time trying to decipher it.

"The last door on the left, don't go near any other room." She waved her hand back towards the back.

After about four minutes passed she swung her legs up on the sofa. "He must have had to shit, with his nasty ass," she mumbled.

She must have dozed off because the next thing she knew something heavy was on her legs and her arms were pinned down above her head. Snapping her eyes open, she saw Zo fumbling with his pants.

"Hell naw, nigga! Get your ass off me!" She bucked her body hard, but his knees had her legs trapped, one against the sofa and the other was under his.

"I'll get off you, after I get me a piece of this. Your ass always walking around like you too good for folks! You give everybody else some, it's my turn now."

Continuing to buck under him, her heart broke when she felt him enter her. If she had been wet, she would have barely felt him, but since she was dry as a desert it hurt. He pushed hard and he just felt nasty inside of her.

"Damn girl, you got some good pussy. I see why Taj drops everything when you call."

His talking just released his bad breath, and that mixed with the blunt he'd smoked made her feel nauseous. Her heart rate kicked up a notch and she knew she had to get out of this.

For the Love of a Boss

"Zo, you don't want to do this. I promise I won't tell Taj if you stop right now!" Her voice cracked with unshed tears.

"What? You think I'm scared of Taj? Shit, this pussy too good to stop." He huffed, blowing more bad air her way.

The more she bucked underneath the harder he went, so she stopped. Closing her eyes, she let her mind take her away from her body. Even with her lying limp this trifling, stanky ass nigga didn't care. When he finished, Kalissa opened her eyes. Then, barely opening her mouth, she let him know how she felt.

"One day I will kill your no-good ass. Don't forget it."

He laughed as he hurriedly clasped his pants together, jumped off her and ran out the door. Kalissa grabbed a beer bottle and followed him. He was almost to his car as she slung the bottle at him. He must have heard it because he turned and moved his head right so that it missed him and cracked against the sidewalk.

Kalissa had barely made it in the house when her stomach churned and she ran to the bathroom, chucking up everything in her stomach. Spit ran down the side of her mouth as she crouched over the toilet. The thought of him being in her bathroom made her heave once again in the toilet, further releasing the bile in her stomach.

Wondering how the hell she got caught up in this situation, her bottom felt wet, reminding her of the feel and smell of Lorenzo. She jerked back from the toilet as she thought of his slimy ass being in her bathroom.

All the years she had known him, Kalissa always thought of him as Taj's sidekick, and though she knew he was a dog, she never thought he would stoop this low. She bumped into Jamila's potty seat as she dragged herself up. Her baby had been in the next room while this maggot took her stuff!

The shower couldn't get hot enough as she tried to scrub herself free of his smell. Scrubbing her pussy until it hurt, she didn't mind the pain the scrub had caused. She was determined to get his funk out of her, so she bathed four times but still smelled his nasty breath. Finally, as the water ran cool, she stepped out only to be assaulted by the smell again.

Ten minutes later, she was deep in bleach. The entire bathroom was scrubbed and totally disinfected. Then it was back to the shower. Neither the bleach nor the hot water could wash away her humiliation. Hot tears cascaded down her face as she hiccupped from holding her emotions in.

She wanted to call Taj, but shame wouldn't let her. She should have known better than to let him inside her apartment and to not smoke with him. It just never crossed her mind that this man she had known since middle school would cross those lines. Racking her brain, she tried to remember if there had been any indicators in the past that he even looked at her that way. Back in the day and even now, the only time she saw him was when she was with Taj. Whenever she saw him alone, she just spoke and kept it moving, because he just wasn't her cup of tea.

Obviously she should have paid more attention to his trifling, ugly, dirty ass. A chill slivered through her chest.

"Arrggghhh!" she screamed in her pillow biting into it so hard she bit the inside of her lower lip.

CHAPTER 8

One month later

"Terika's not coming in tonight. Do you think you can get somebody else to help close?" Torrey, her manager, asked her.

With a heavy breath, Kalissa nodded, then as usual her mouth took over. "Isn't Tammy supposed to make sure I have a closer?" She widened her eyes innocently.

Tammy was the front-end supervisor. She was fat, lazy and full of white privilege. Ever since Kalissa had moved up to 'night' supervisor, she handled more of Tammy's responsibilities than her own. Tammy called it training, but it was just funny that this "training" seemed to be everything Tammy didn't want to do. It wasn't a problem because if things worked out, Kalissa would soon have her job. More money and all day shift hours. Ever since the incident with Zo, she had concentrated on work and Jamila, so she knew she was ready for the job.

"There's a lot that Tammy should be doing, but she doesn't," Torrey said under his breath.

In order to see the schedule she leaned in close, when her breast touched his shoulder, she jumped back, "As long as you know that. I can't do anything about it, but you can."

Before the 'incident' she would have tried him, but she just felt dirty and shamed. As ridiculous as it was, it felt like if she got too close to people they could smell the dirt and feel her shame. She knew Torrey was interested, because he always breathed a little heavier when she was around and gave her the look. He was older, not by much, and kind of stocky, but he was cute and next in line to be district manager. Kalissa had thought about trying him, since every woman in the restaurant wanted him, but the bile that rose in her throat each time she thought about it stopped her.

If she could kill Zo and get away with it, she would. Not only had her taken her body without her permission, he took her confidence and swagger away from her.

"Hey, are you alright?" Torrey touched her arm as he spoke softly.

"Yeah, I'm okay, I was just trying to think of who I can get to close," she replied, moving her arm away.

"Okay, but if you need to talk to me about anything, you know I'm here for you," he said softly.

"Thanks, but I'm good." She backed out of the office, throwing the words over her shoulder.

Ever since the 'incident', she couldn't stand to be touched unless she initiated it, which wasn't happening. If nothing else, Kalissa realized that she had been too trusting and naïve. Never again.

Frustrated with her weakness, she shook her head. When she passed through the kitchen, the harsh smell of fish hit her nose. Everything she had eaten rushed up her throat and she had barely made it to the bathroom when she threw up.

The closest thing to her was toilet tissue. Kalissa used it to wipe her mouth while she looked at the ceiling, tears bubbling in her eyes.

"Lord, no! Please don't let this happen to me," she whispered. Looking at her uniform, she noticed specks of vomit on the front. It almost had her heaving again.

After she cleaned up, she walked out the bathroom and ran into Brian. He wasn't as mean to her now, but he still wasn't the friendliest. He grabbed her arm to keep her from falling since he almost mowed her down.

"Are you alright?" His voice was deep with concern, but his calloused hands almost made her throw up again.

She snatched her arm away, nodded and walked off. She didn't even notice how he watched her until she disappeared into the kitchen.

The rest of the night passed in a blur. All she could think about was going home and getting into bed. Since this wasn't her first rodeo, she knew what the nausea, sore breast and being tired all the time meant, but she prayed hard every day that it wasn't true.

After helping the one closing server clean up, she trudged home with every muscle in her body aching. The one good thing was, Jamila was spending the night with her sister, so she would get to sleep to some extent.

No such luck after five hours; she awakened to her entire room smelling like the restaurant, which only made her sick. Enough was enough!

Forty-five minutes later, after a hot shower, brushing her teeth and washing her face, she was at the Rite-Aid two blocks from where her sister lived. She knew with her hair in a ponytail, sweats and a tee shirt on, that she looked like a bum, but she didn't care.

"Lissa! What's wrong with you? Are you sick?" her sister Mahali shrieked as soon as she walked in.

"Nope, I'm just tired. One of the servers called out last night, the closer at that, so I had to do my job and hers." There was no way that she would confide in Mahali her suspicions. The entire family would know before she backed out of the driveway.

Jamila ran from the bedroom and tackled her legs.

"Momma! What took you so long?" she cried.

The happiness in her daughter's eyes hit her heart like a sledgehammer. If her suspicions were true, there was no way she would take away from her beloved child to try to feed a child from that bastard.

"You know if you ever want to get a man, you need to take a little more care with your looks before you walk out of the house," her sister slid in sarcastically.

An eye roll masked how hard that rebuke hit her, she shot back, "You know Mahali, everybody's main goal in life is not to catch a man. Considering I've worked over twenty hours in the past two days, you think I care about how I look to come pick up my child?"

"I'm just saying. Even if that isn't your goal, you could try to put more effort in your looks."

"Come on, Jamila, let's go. Thanks for keeping her," she said dismissively over her shoulder.

"No problem. Oh, by the way, you should call momma, she called asking about you and Jamila. She also said you weren't answering her calls."

"I'll call her. I didn't answer because I was working."

Kalissa would call her mother eventually, but not today. She and her mother had a tense relationship at times. Her mom had left her dad to raise her and her knee baby sister all by himself, and Kalissa was a pre-teen at the time, so she suffered immensely from the divorce. At the time, she was in between being a tomboy and becoming a young lady, so her lady skills lacked from it. It wasn't something she thought about often, but when her mom wanted to nitpick her to death, that resentment came out. So there were times they got along and moments they didn't.

"Momma! Aunt Mahali painted my toenails! Look," her baby yelled as soon as they got in the car.

As big of a tomboy that Lissa had been while growing up, she was blessed with a girly-girl for a daughter. Jamila always wanted the dresses, patent leather shoes, jewelry, painted nails and toes. The exact opposite of her momma growing up.

"I see, baby, they're so pretty."

When they got home, her sister's words pounded in her head. While Jamila played in her room, she looked in the mirror. Her hair was jet black and her ponytail hung down to the middle of her back, but her deep-set eyes had dark circles under them, and her thick eyebrows needed to be arched. The oversized sweats and tee shirt hung off her, as every clothes of hers did, unless it was size zero, or she got them out of the kid's department.

Once Kalissa down to her undies, she was disappointed as usual with her small frame. Small tits and a little bump for a butt that looked decent in fitted clothes. Glancing down at her arms, she flinched at the scars that lined them. Jamila saved her from going down that rabbit hole.

"Momma, you naked!" her baby screamed with laughter.

She threw on her robe, swept up her baby, and they played with toys until it was time for her to cook and get Jamila in bed.

Once her daughter was asleep and her little shabby apartment was clean, she took the pregnancy test kit out of her purse. Her hand shook.

Instead of the recommended three minutes, Kalissa waited five. Her eyes widened and her heart sped up when she saw the plus sign.

C.D. Blue

CHAPTER 9

"Nope, can't be right," she muttered as she filled her thirty-two ounce cup with more water. After thirty minutes, she tried it again with the same results

Everything blurred in front of her as tears filled her eyes and her throat closed. The only person that had been inside her was that nasty slimy Zo! Just when she felt she was putting her life together by moving up at work, not smoking dope, and staying to herself. Now this!

Steadying herself on the bathroom sink, her entire body shook. *Think, Kalissa, think!*

"Umm, umm, umm," she hummed uncontrollably.

When she found out she was pregnant with Jamila, an abortion never crossed her mind and from the moment she found out Terry's seed was growing inside her, there was an instant connection. Terry had wanted her to have an abortion, but she knew she was having her baby with or without him! But not this nasty seed!

If she had been foolish enough to have unprotected sex with anyone, she would consider having the child. But Zo had taken her pussy with his nasty, ugly ass! Ugh!

"Only you, Lissa, only you," she murmured to herself as she automatically began cleaning the tub of Jamila's little dirty streaks.

Once that was complete, she went to kitchen, grabbed a beer out of the fridge and sat on the sofa. Taking a long swig out of her Michelob, she laid her head back and closed her eyes. Images flooded her head of how many ways she could kill Zo and get away with it. In one scene she slit his throat and watched him gurgle to his death, then in another she caught him on the street and pushed him in front of a semi-truck and watched his body implode.

She shook the evil thoughts partly out of her mind because had to come up with a solution before it was too late. She thought about her bills and how little she would have left after paying her bills. Asking her dad was out of the question. He would give it to her, no doubt, but he would require a detailed explanation as to why she needed it. There was no way she was telling him what happened. He had been shattered when she had gotten pregnant with Jamila!

There was only one person she knew she could get the money from: Taj.

Breathing hard, she thought of many lies she could tell him as to why she needed it. Settling with the idea of telling him her electricity was getting cut off, she threw on some grey sweats a tee shirt, pulled her hair back into a ponytail and put on her New Balance athletic shoes. Jamila was fast asleep when she checked on her, before knocking on her neighbor's door.

Her neighbor, a nice lady in her thirties, opened the door with a huge smile.

"Hey, Kalissa! Come on in. You want something to drink?"

"Uh, no, not tonight. I was wondering if your daughter could sit with Jamila for a little while. She's asleep," she added the last part after noticing the puzzled look on her neighbor's face.

"Is everything alright?"

"Yeah, I just forgot to get some snacks for her to take to school tomorrow and I need to run to Walmart," the lie fell effortlessly off her tongue.

"Oh, okay. I'll send her over. I'm sure she's back there on the phone. You know how these teenagers are," the woman said with a laugh.

"Okay, thanks." Kalissa turned away and walked back into her apartment.

"Kalissa? You know if you ever need to talk, I'm here for you."

"Thanks, but I'm okay, just tired from working and being forgetful." She managed a small smile.

Sitting on the edge of the couch, she waited impatiently for the teenager to come. It only took about ten minutes, but it felt more like a couple of hours. She was ready to get this over with.

Instructions were given and she flew out the door. Heading down Fairview Avenue, she drove past the decay of the west side into the old money of Cloverdale.

Stuck at a red light, a loud car pulled up beside her. It was an Impala sitting high on some twenty-fours, painted a flashy metallic bronze with gold rims. The driver motioned for her to roll her window down. He had shoulder length dreads with gold tips that reflected nicely off his dark chocolate skin. He smiled shyly, showing a hint of gold.

"Hey, ma. What's up?"

"Not much. How're you?"

"I'm good, but I'd be better if I could call you sometimes. You got a man?"

"Nah, but this isn't a good time." Her situation along came crashing back to the forefront of her mind. Giving the traffic lights a side eye, she was ready to roll.

Before she knew what was happening, he was standing at her window, handing her a card. His arms were cut and she knew that he had a six pack under his tee shirt; she drooled inwardly.

"When the time gets better, give me a call. You too pretty to pass up. I'm Rollo."

Gently taking the card, she smiled at him. "I'm Kalissa, nice meeting you." Seeing green in her peripheral vision, she gave a small wave and pulled off.

Rollo was on her mind as she rode slowly into Taj's apartment complex. Tucked away off the road, the trees lining the street exuded peace instead of creepiness. The apartments were nondescript and brown on the outside, but she knew they cost a fortune. The main occupants were rich white college kids, who had parents that could foot their monthly bills. It was close to the private Huntingdon College, and no matter how wild parties got on this side of town, no one got hurt, nor was it splashed across the news.

Taj fit in perfectly. He was so clean-cut and preppy. No one suspected him of anything; he even had her dad fooled!

Double clicking her key fob to make sure her car was locked once she parked, she almost bumped into two young jocks, one of whom gave her a once-over and nodded.

"Hey," she said hurriedly.

"We were hoping you were looking for us," one of them said loudly.

Kalissa stopped and with one eyebrow raised, looked back, then decided it wasn't worth it. Both of them were cute, but white guys had never been her type.

Taj lived on the second floor and the stairway was lit, but the stairs were steep as hell. If she had thought about it, she would have worn heels instead and her problem would have been solved.

Knocking loudly, the soft tendrils of music floated through the closed door.

The door was snatched opened and Taj stood right there looking sharp in a white tee shirt paired with white jeans and some fly white Adidas.

"Lissa! What are you doing here?" He looked surprised.

"Can I come in?"

"Yeah, you know you can." He stepped to the side to let her in.

His good looks changed in her eyes once she saw Zandra draped across the couch. She had on a short metallic skirt, with a white blouse that was unbuttoned down to her belly to reveal a matching metallic bra. Lissa rolled her eyes.

"Hey to you too. What you doing coming over here looking like a bag lady?" Zandra said, sarcasm and jealousy dripping in her tone.

"I still look better than you, even on my bag lady days, so why you worried about it?"

"Bitch, you wish."

"Nah, hoe, I know and you do too. Anyway, Taj, can I talk to you in private?"

"Hell no! How you gonna insult me, then think you can talk to my man privately? Say what you need to say." Zandra had sat up with her nostrils flaring.

"I wish y'all would stop this shit! Lissa, is it really that personal?" Taj yelled.

"Yep, it is."

Taj looked torn between granting an audience with Kalissa and focusing his attention on his girlfriend. Zandra's body language dared him, but he knew Lissa wouldn't have bust in on him if it wasn't important.

"Come on back to the room," he said quietly, while grabbing Lissa's arm.

"I can't believe this shit! Taj, are you seriously taking her to the bedroom? With me sitting right here?"

"Zandra, shut up! Yeah, I am. This is my muthafuckin' house, sit your ass down until I come back up."

"Keep playing with me," Zandra muttered as she settled back on the sofa.

Taj led her down his long hallway, passing two closed doors. The lights were out, which made the hallway seem longer. It felt like her long walk of shame.

"What's up, Lissa? And this shit better be important, 'cuz now I'ma have to hear her fuckin' mouth all night."

Lissa looked around Taj's bedroom. The decor was all black, with a zebra print comforter. Black and white pictures lined the wall, black curtains adorned the windows, and a plush white Persian rug graced the floor. It was all nice, tasteful, and a huge upgrade from his bedroom at his parents' house.

"You know I wouldn't have come over here if it wasn't important." Now that it was time to talk, she felt uncertain. She didn't know how he would react, or how much to tell him. Zo was his cousin after all.

"Well?" The tips of Taj's nose flared as he stared at her.

"Look, I'm sorry I bust in on you like this, but I need to borrow some money." She looked at him imploringly.

Taj's face softened slightly. "What's going on? Your lights getting turned off or does Jamila need something? You could have called me for that, you know I got you." His tone hardened at the last part.

"No, I need to get an abortion." Out of nowhere, her voice cracked and tears sprang into her eyes.

Taj moved closer and grabbed her hands.

"That nigga Terry, again? I thought you was through with him. I mean I can loan it to you, but that fat ass nigga need to shit or get his big ass off the pot. How much longer are y'all—"

"It's not Terry! Zo raped me!" Big hot tears escaped her eyes.

He released her hands while the different stages of emotions ran across his face. Disbelief, hurt and anger all showed in a span of a few minutes.

"My cousin? What the fuck you talking about Lissa?" Raising his voice while still shaking his head. "Nah, I must have misunderstood you, cuz I know damn well you didn't say my cousin *raped* you? Fuck naw!"

"He did, Taj! He came by my apartment one night looking for you, then he asked me if I wanted to burn one. I knew I shouldn't have let his ass in, but I never thought he would do me like that!" Covering her face, the shame burnt through her body and shook her entire core.

She felt Taj's warm embrace before she fully recognized what was going on. Just the closeness, the heat and the care, made her tears come harder and her body shook uncontrollably. She felt safe. This was her best friend, the one person who knew every bit of her, every bone, hair follicle and leftover tissues of all her skeletons.

"Tell me what happened." His voice sounded strangled in her hair. She told him from the beginning to end, not only what happened but down to what that trifling low down nigga had on.

Taj never let go, he held on tighter and she held him just as tight. All her worries and fears melted because she knew he had her back. Finally releasing her, he wiped his face with one hand and his expression had changed.

"Don't worry, I got you. Just make the appointment and let me know, 'cuz I'ma take you to it."

"Nah, you don't have to do that," she said, but her heart hoped he wouldn't pay her any attention.

"Gurl, the hell you say! Ain't no way I'ma let you go through this by yourself. You've been through enough by yourself as it is."

Wiping her tears with the bottom of her shirt, she nodded. "I'm going home now. I'll leave you to deal with the bamboo in the front. Sorry I messed your night up."

"You didn't mess up anything. I just wish you woulda told me sooner. Don't worry about Zandra, she'll be alright. And I promise you, I'll deal with Zo's ass."

"Humph, I wasn't worried about her no way. I give zero fucks about how she feels." Her hand was on the doorknob when she turned.

"Taj?'

"Yeah." He looked up with red-rimmed eyes.

"Thank you for always being here for me. I appreciate you more than I can ever show you."

Seeing him blush through his anger made her smile, as she walked out the room feeling much lighter than she had arrived.

***

Zandra was steaming! Stomping into the kitchen, she swung the refrigerator door open so hard she almost tore off the hinges. She and Taj had been doing great lately and she felt as if she was closer to moving in with him. She wanted out of her parents' house and for all the hoes in the street to know that she was the real bitch!

It was no surprise that Kalissa would try to come between them, waltzing in his house with sweats and a tee shirt, acting like she was some kind of queen. Zandra couldn't stand her ass! It never failed that every time she came around, Taj would disrespect her and put Lissa before her. Frowning as she glanced down the hallway, she heard murmurings, and she wanted to put her ear against the door to hear what the hell they were talking about.

Grabbing the bottle of wine, she nixed that idea. With her luck, Taj would come out and then that would be another problem. Settling on the sofa with her glass, her foot tapped a hole in the floor.

The creak of the bedroom door opening made her sit straight up, and her fake nonchalant look turned into a mean mug when she saw it was Kalissa. She sauntered through the living room with a smirk before leaving without saying a word to Zandra.

It took Taj a few minutes to appear. She couldn't decipher his look, but he cut her off as she opened her mouth to let him know how she felt about what happened.

"Look, I know you're mad, but it was truly an emergency."

"It's always an emergency with her." Zandra rolled her eyes. "That still doesn't excuse how you talked to me in front of her."

Taj bucked his eyes, "You was wrong for the shit you said, Zandra. All you had to do was speak to her. You could have left it at that."

Zandra stood, ready to fight. "You always taking up for that bum bitch! I keep telling you her main objective is to break us up. And you gonna keep on and let it happen."

"Don't let that liquid courage get you fucked up! Lissa is my friend; she don't care if we're together or not. You wanting me to give up a friendship I've had since I was twelve is what's gonna be the end for us."

The fire she saw in his eyes made her settle back down on the sofa. "Hmm, you just think she doesn't care because she has you fooled."

"Whatever, Zandra," Taj said.

With his back to her, he rolled a blunt on the bar. No matter how mad he made her, he still looked so fine and his money made him even finer, in her eyes.

"Anyway, what did she want that was so damn important?"

"I'm not telling you her business. The real question is why do you seem to hate her so much? Y'all used to be best friends."

It stung, that he wouldn't share what Kalissa wanted, but she played it off. "I don't hate her," Zandra spoke softly, walking towards him.

Taj looked at her through a cloud of smoke. "It seems like it. Every time she calls, you get mad. Tonight you insulted her as soon as she walked in the door. You shole don't like her."

Taking the blunt from him, she pulled on it hard before she answered. "That's because you put her before everybody."

"No, I don't. I have her back because I know she has mine."

Zandra had a coughing fit as the smoke went down the wrong way. Taj patted her back as he laughed her.

"Kalissa doesn't give a shit about anybody except her child. What she does is, manipulate people to benefit herself. Like I said, she has you fooled."

"Naw, you're just saying that 'cuz y'all fell out. When y'all was close you didn't feel that way. I know that's not true 'cuz when my momma put me out, she was the only who would take me in. Everybody else just came up with excuses."

She looked at him, noticing how tight his eyes had gotten, and he almost looked angry.

"I'm sure she got something out of it. I knew that she could be cold to some people. I just didn't realize that applied to everybody until after we fell out. All it takes is to do something she doesn't like. The only thing she's ever done based on emotions is, have Jamila. Don't worry. One day you find out what the rest of us had to learn the hard way."

"What's that?"

"That bitch doesn't have a soul."

C.D. Blue

CHAPTER 10

Taj left Cedric, Desi and Duke in the car, while he finished talking business with the owner of the Mom and Pop Convenience store on Narrow Lane Road. He had showed them a small storage area in the back of the store that could be accessed from the outside, and could be theirs. For the right price.

Ishaan and Kabir were the Indian brothers that owned the store. They had never been robbed, an encounter that made them tolerate no fooling around in their store. It probably helped that they both carried firearms and kept a rifle behind the counter.

After conferring with his three riders, Taj negotiated a price which included a monthly fee, along with buying shipments of women's sanitary pads and tampons to fill the small room. Just in case anyone looked.

When he got back in his car, his three passengers were bobbing their heads to some track from a local artist. Since it was someone they knew, they were giving dude major props, but it didn't sound like much to Taj. Putting things in perspective, he knew it was time to deal with Zo, so he couldn't get his mind right until that was accomplished.

"Hey, man, where's Zo? I thought he would have been with us to look at the spot?" Cet seemed to have read his mind.

"Nah, not this time. But I need you to come with me to handle a lil' business." Taj kept his eyes on the road as he spoke to Cet.

"A'ight, that's what's up."

"Where y'all want me to drop y'all at?" Taj looked through his rearview mirror and caught the eye of Duke.

"Tee, we need to peep as much as we can on the business side. Maybe we should ride out with y'all," Desi said.

"I got you, cuz, but this is a little personal. Don't worry, I'ma keep you up in the game."

"Fasho! That's what's up, man. You can drop us off at ASU, we need to get rid of this product anyways."

"Aye, man. See if your connect can get us more Mollys. That shit be selling like crazy! Especially at the parties." Desi's voice was loud with excitement.

That one comment not only sparked an idea in Taj's head, but also made him realize that he was making the right choice in what he was about to do.

"Yeah, I'll double my re-up. How much weed they be smoking at these parties?" Taj needed to know because he stayed out of the mix when it came to the social scenes. Especially with the college crowd. He would see some of his old classmates and always felt the shame of not making his mom proud by getting his education.

"Here at ASU? A lot! Here they want weed and blow. Now when you go to the white schools they'll smoke weed, but they be wanting pills and powder! All the time, whether it's a party or not. You can take that shit anywhere!" He laughed as he and his brother dabbed it up.

Taj turned left into the entrance of the university and pulled in by the dining hall. "A'ight, we gonna meet up soon and work out a plan. Y'all about to expand some and get your dough up."

No sooner had the brothers got of the car than Taj heard someone calling their name. That let him know they were on top of their game. Impressed, he nodded.

He and Cet hadn't made it half a mile before Cet started asking questions.

"A'ight, mane, where we going?"

"I need to get with Zo right quick," Taj answered, glancing at his passenger.

Raising his eyebrows slightly, Cet mumbled, "A'ight."

"Look, man, you gonna have to take Zo's slack until we come up with a plan. That also means you get his money too."

"Hold up! Zo ain't with us no mo'?"

"That's why we going over there, I'ma make that shit official."

Cet blew into his fist, "That nigga been stealing, ain't he? I knew that nigga was a thief, I knew it!"

"Nah, but he did some grimy shit that I can't let slide, jus' follow my lead when we get there."

Okay, cool, I'm wit' whatever." Cet bopped his head to "I'm A DBoy" by Lil' Wayne.

They rolled into the projects and Taj paid no attention to the few people that tried to flag him down. After two left turns, they turned into Zo's parking lot, and Taj dodged the potholes until he found a decent parking space.

"I don't see his car," Cet observed, looking around.

"Ureka probably has it. His ass better be here. I told him I was coming to pick up my money."

Taking the stairs two at a time, Taj double knocked on the door, while Cet walked slowly, taking in the surroundings. There were a few youngsters that worked for Zo, hanging around the parking lot. Other than that, it was pretty quiet.

Zo answered the door with a dirty yellow tee shirt, sleep still in his eyes and crust around his mouth.

"Damn cuz, I didn't know you meant right this fucking minute you was coming," Zo complained as he moved to the back of the apartment.

Looking around, Taj couldn't understand how anyone lived in such filth. There were dishes on the coffee table, the sofa and the end tables. One end table had a glass of milk that had split. There was an overwhelming smell of roaches. Just nasty.

Cet had finally made it in and they heard Zo's feet sliding across the linoleum before they saw him. He was carrying a gray duffel bag. He sneered when he saw Cedric.

"I didn't know you had this circus looking muthafucka wit' you. What up, shrimp?"

"At least I ain't living in no circus," Cet muttered.

"What you say?" Zo growled.

He threw the duffel at Taj's feet. Taj moved it closer to the door and when he straightened he jabbed Zo in the mouth. Zo stumbled back, holding his mouth.

"What the fuck? Mane, what the hell is wrong with you?"

Taj led with another jab, then followed with a cross so quick Zo fell back on the coffee table knocking half the trash off of it.

"You fucked up, Zo! Why the hell you did that shit to Lissa?"

Zo looked at him and laughed while wiping the blood off his lip with his left hand.

"What? Wait, you tripping about *that* bitch? I ought to whoop your ass coming at me like that, nigga. You crazy."

Realization lit in Zo's eyes as he laughed. "Oh, I know what's up. You mad 'cuz I got some before you."

A myriad of reflections passed through Taj's mind. He saw red, then the hurt; no, the damage that had been done to Kalissa blinded him.

"Nigga, you violated her! She didn't give you shit!" Taj roared before he went at Zo again. Zo countered two of his punches with his arm, before he hit Taj in the eye.

Falling back, Taj rolled on the balls of his feet and kept one arm up to deflect the next punch from Zo. Mustering all of his anger, he dotted him in the nose and felt the cartilage burst before the blood began pouring out.

"Aaggh! Nigga you broke my nose!" Zo roared, coming at him.

Taj threw a left hook right at his forehead and laid him out. Cet walked over and rained more blows on Zo then finished him off with three hard kicks to his ribs.

Zo yelled and put his hand under the sofa cushion as if to lift himself up. Quicker than a flash, Cet had his revolver out with the hammer cocked.

"Mane, don't make me splatter the few brains cells you got on this floor. I don't even need another reason, I'll do it for fun." Cet said calmly. He wasn't even out of breath.

Zo scowled from him to Taj, but he moved his hand to the floor.

"You gonna regret this bitch move, cuz, I promise you will," Said Zo.

"I ain't regretting shit! If you wasn't my blood I would kill yo' monkey ass. From now on you are on your muthafuckin'

88

own! I'm done fucking wit' you, I put that on everythang I love. Come on, Cet, let's get the fuck outta here."

Taj picked up the duffel. Meanwhile, Cet kept his hammer trained on Zo, walking backwards.

As bad as his eye was stinging, Taj pulled out of the parking lot quickly after they got into the car; he wasn't taking no chances on Zo coming out of the apartment blazing. He knew his cousin and he knew he would have to watch his back.

"Mane, Zo raped Lissa?" Cet's leg was bouncing up and down and hurt rang in his tone.

"Yeah, but don't let on to her that you know, she's real private like that."

Cet nodded. "No worries, but on a real tip, it's my respect for you that kept that nigga from getting a bullet between his eyes. I promise you that."

Taj nodded as they made it down the Western Boulevard in silence.

CHAPTER 11

Questioning herself for the fiftieth time on whether her upcoming abortion was the right thing to do, Kalissa blew out her breath. Her appointment was the next day. Suddenly, guilt filled every pore in her body. Reaching for her Michelob Light on the counter, she shook her head. What she was drinking was proof enough that she needed to make the appointment. All she wanted was beer and weed, a testament that she was carrying the devil's child.

Jamila was in the bed, and it seemed as if she had been an extra handful lately, but it probably more so because Kalissa was tired. Extremely tired. Another sign that this was the spawn of Lucifer in her belly.

Reaching deep into the sudsy dishwater, she grabbed the last of the silverware at the bottom, washed it, drained the water and was about to clean out the sink, when a knock sounded at the door.

Looking at the door suspiciously, because Taj and Fefe had left a few hours earlier and they were the only two people she knew who came unannounced. Tiptoeing to the door, her heart slammed in her chest when she saw Zo. He knocked again, so hard this time that she jumped.

"Nah, not this time nigga," she muttered, stomping back to the kitchen.

Grabbing her butcher knife, she heard him yelling.

"Lissa! Open this damn door! I ain't leaving until you do, with yo' snitching ass."

Boom! Boom! Boom!

"Bitch, open this door!"

Knowing he was less than two feet away, her nose filled with his funk. Flashes of him covering her body, filling her with his stanky seed, sent a chill through her body, piercing her heart.

She clutched the knife tighter to her chest and played out the best scenario, because she was going to kill his ass! She pictured herself opening the door with the chain on it and sliding the knife through his heart. With her hand on the knob, she heard someone running up the steps.

"What tha fuck? Nigga . . ." Zo's voice was strangled.

Too curious not to know, but not crazy enough to open the door, she looked out the peephole. Zo had his hands up, looking pissed off.

Kalissa cracked open the door and there stood Cet with that big ass gun, holding Zo hostage.

"If you don' get yo' punk ass from around this do', nigga . . ." Cedric talked between gritted teeth.

"So it's like that, huh? Errybody want save this hoe? Damn! Her pussy ain't that good."

The only sound was the hammer of the gun being cocked.

"I ain't gonna say it again, take yo' muthafuckin' broke ass on, nigga! The only reason you still breathin' is 'cuz you Tee's blood." Cedric's voice was low, but carried his intentions.

Zo slid by him, sneering, "This ain't over, my nigga. You caught me slipping this time, but best believe it won't happen again. You's a dead man."

"Bet, my nigga. See me in da streets."

Cedric stayed on the top steps until Kalissa heard the roar of Zo's raggedy muffler leave the parking lot.

"Cedric? What the hell were you doing out here?" She was glad he came, but he was the last person she expected to see.

"Uhh, Taj kinda told me to watch out for you, uh, you know since Zo isn't wit' us no mo'" Cedric stuttered and stammered as she stared at him.

"Okay, I gotcha. Well, it's good looking out. I'm going to bed. Maybe you should go home."

"I am," he smiled, her porch light reflecting off the gold in his mouth.

Starting down the steps, his head popped back up before she closed the door. "Uhh . . . Kalissa? You might want to sharpen that knife if you using it for protection."

She had forgotten that she still held onto the knife. Laughing, she put it behind her back as she waved him off. Part of her felt as if she should have invited him in, but that's how she landed in her current predicament. No more playing nice with these niggas.

Turning out the lights, she didn't even bother to look to see if he was still out there. Internally, she was afraid that Zo would come back and hurt Cedric, but after glancing at her baby sleeping soundly, that was not her problem.

***

"Mommy, I'm hungry, wake up!" Jamila's voice was high pitched.

"Umph, okay," she said.

The beer didn't taste as good in the morning as it did the night before. She dragged herself out of the bed and managed to make her baby some pancakes before getting her dressed for daycare. When Taj knocked at the door, early, of course, she tried to play it cool, but butterflies filled her stomach. He walked in looking uncomfortable.

"Unca Tee!" Jamila ran to him.

He picked her up and spun her around. While they played, Kalissa gathered Jamila's bag, turned off the lights and walked back up front with a fake smile.

"Let's do this."

After dropping her baby off at daycare, they made it to the clinic in fifteen minutes, mostly in silence. Her stomach lurched once they parked. Since they were early, they just sat there. Taj was the only drug dealer that ran his life like an army sergeant. He was meticulous to the core.

"You, alright?" Taj asked.

"Yeah, I'm good," she lied.

"I know your ass nervous, but I'm wit' you, don't forget that." He put his hand on the door handle.

"Wait a minute! You talked to Cedric?"

Taj looked down, clearly uneasy. "Yeah, he called me last night."

"I know he wasn't just riding by and I know he wanted to know why you asked him to watch after me." She blew out a harsh breath. "I really don't know how to feel about it. On one hand I'm glad, but the on the other I feel like I should be pissed off."

Taj looked at her with his eyebrows raised. "Look, Lissa, I didn't mean to tell him. He was with me when I confronted Zo and it slipped out. You know damn well I wouldn't betray you like that. I didn't tell him about this, tho'." He gestured towards the clinic.

"Humph, it's cool, I guess. Like I said he saved me last night. I ain't gonna lie, I was scareder than a mug."

"Yea, I'm glad he was there too, 'cuz I didn't tell him to watch out for you. He did that shit on his own."

"Fa real? Humph, might be something to that lil' ass nigga," she smiled brilliantly at her friend. "He just grew three inches, that quick."

"You so wrong. I'm glad he was there, tho'. I don't know what Zo what was thinking." Taj shook his head.

"I don't either, but thank you for always being here, I mean that." Her words were softly spoken with a slight smile.

Taj knew how hard it was for Lissa to speak her emotions, but she always showed loyalty and care. This was one reason he paid Zandra's bad omens about her no attention.

"You ready to do this?"

"Yep, even if I'm not, let's go!"

The Willinest Clinic was divided into two buildings, the front one was for regular appointments and the abortion clinic was in the back. When they walked around, there were people standing around, who rushed to them as soon as they came into view.

"Honey, you don't have to do this," an older woman spoke urgently, trying to shove a pamphlet in her hand.

"Don't do the devil's work! You'll go to hell!" another woman cried.

"This is murder! Do you really want to murder your child?" a white man with blotchy skin said harshly, blocking their path.

"Nah, what's gonna be murda is, if you don't move yo' cracker ass out my way," Taj dared the man.

For the Love of a Boss

The man came to his senses and moved while still mumbling about murdering an innocent child. Taj grabbed her hand and pulled her towards the front door. She was at a near run to keep with him.

"Damn! Can they do that?"

"I'on know, them folks crazy," Taj answered as the cool air hit them once they made it inside.

There was a person behind a window that they had to show their ID to. After they checked for her name, they buzzed them into the lobby. An extra skinny lady stood when they entered.

"I saw what happened! I'm so sorry, but we can only make them stay so many feet away from the building." She gushed on and on.

Getting Kalissa signed in, the woman gave Taj a funny look when he pulled out the cash to pay; she didn't say anything though. She and Taj sat in the waiting area until her name was called. Taj squeezed her hand before she walked back to the back.

She clenched her hands, willing her mind to shut down. The antiseptic smell that assaulted her as soon as she made it to the back got stuck in her nose as they took her vitals. By the time she changed into the skimpy gown they gave her, she had gone to another place mentally, and stayed there.

It was almost as if being in a dream. She saw the doctor, heard him, but barely comprehended the words. Nodding slowly, it wasn't until the vacuum sound and the slight pull, maybe imagined, of her insides being disconnected from her body, did she shake back to reality.

It was over. A nurse wheeled her on the bed to a separate area, handed her two pills and a little cup of water. Kalissa closed her eyes but the vacuum sound haunted her. With no idea of time, it seemed as if only minutes had passed before she was led back to the locker that held her clothes and was given a sanitary napkin. Once dressed, it still seemed as if there was an internal fog inside the clinic, everything had an unreal tint to it.

Taj was still in the same seat, looking worried when she opened the door. Giving him a reassuring smile, she took care of the follow-up appointment and met him at the door.

"Are you okay?"

"Yeah, I'm a little light-headed, but I'll be okay."

"You always say you're okay, even when you ain't," he muttered.

He grabbed her hand again and they walked along the sidewalk. Taj walked slower this time, but his posture and steps conveyed that he was not to be fucked with. No one approached them.

"I'ma take you home, but I'll pick up Jamila from daycare later. I've gotta take care of some business right quick."

Nodding, Kalissa looked out the window, still not totally connected to reality. She just wanted to sleep.

***

After making sure that Lissa was comfortable, because he knew she wasn't okay, Taj drove out to Hope Hull to see his uncle. The text came in while he was in the waiting room at the clinic. Knowing he didn't owe any money, he checked his notebook to be sure and it wasn't time for a re-up, so he was clueless as to what this meeting was about.

Hope Hull was right outside of the city. It was more country and had absolutely nothing but homes. Nice homes, but that was it. Going through all the twists and turns, he finally made it to his uncle's home.

Uncle James lived in a ranch style home that screamed simplicity, but Taj knew better. His uncle was the connect for the entire city and surrounding areas. He owned four or five beauty and barber shops, five package stores, along with rental homes. Yet, he chose not to flaunt it.

His aunt opened the door and the aroma of food hit his nose and stomach at the same time. He heard a television blaring from the back of the house.

"Hey, baby, he's out back waiting for you. Are you hungry?" She didn't wait for response. "I'll bring you a plate outside."

Taj walked through the house, marveling at the interior. Simple on the outside, the inside was nothing but extravagance. Polished real wood floors with old heavy furniture. Souvenirs from the many countries they visited lined the walls and tabletops. Not shot glasses, but paintings, artifacts, throws, and knick knacks. The expensive ones.

His uncle was on the patio talking on the phone with a cigarette hanging out his mouth. He acknowledged Taj with a nod towards a chair.

"Naw, if she can't bring her ass to work, give her booth to someone else! No matter how good she is, business is business. A'ight."

He hung up and he looked at Taj for a long minute. Uncle James was a tall lanky man. Milk chocolate skin, he always kept a beard to cover an old knife scar that went from his ear down to his chin.

"What's up, Unc'?" Taj squirmed in his seat because his uncle had that look he'd dished out to him many times in his life. None of them were good times.

"What the hell is goin' on with you and Zo?"

Letting a deep breath escape, Taj moved to the edge of his seat. "Unc', he did some real grimy shit, so I let him go. That's all."

Uncle James stubbed his cigarette out in the ashtray. "Was he stealing?"

"Naw, he just pulled some bitch ass nigga shit. Anyway ain't no real loss 'cuz Zo don't want to get no real money anyway."

"Ump. He said it was over a hoe. Tee, you got to separate the business from personal," James said heatedly.

With a wave of the hand, Taj said, determined to clear things up. "Hell naw! You need to tell that same shit to Zo! He hurt someone close to me to get back at me 'cuz I made Cedric my second-in-command. I did that 'cuz Zo wasn't handling his business. He the only hoe ass I know."

His uncle lit another cigarette while staring out at his expansive backyard. They were interrupted by his aunt bringing food, a soda and a tray out to him.

"Thanks," he smiled at her, looking down at the fried chicken, mashed potatoes, collard greens, and corn bread.

Waiting until she was back in the house, his uncle spoke.

"I trust your judgement, Tee. That's why I put you in charge, but I can't leave him out there hanging. I'll deal with him and if he can't handle it, I'll put him out there with someone else. I just need you to stay out of his area, let him do his thang. He'll either sink or swim."

"What's his area?"

A map miraculously appeared from the bottom half of the wicker table. "This is how my connect wants me to split the city, so we can see who to give more business to. Since you won't touch crack, there will be some overlapping, but I think it will work out."

"Why don't you just introduce me to your connect? That way I'm one less headache for you?" Taj said with a mouth full of food.

Slumping back in his chair with his eyes buck, James took a pull off his cigarette. "Tee, man, you trying to get me kilt! I'm not even one hunnid sure who he is. This man so paranoid, I've known people that have disappeared for trying that shit! And that was just having someone else meet the middle man. Naw, that won't work."

"Damn! Never mind then."

"Just enjoy your food. I'll handle Zo. I just wanted to make sure he wasn't stealing."

Wiping his mouth, he polished off the drumstick and drank the rest of his soda before rising. "I've gotta run and get wit Cet, before I pick up Jamila."

"Who's Jamila? A new chick?"

"Naw, that's Lissa's baby. I promised I'd pick her up from daycare."

"Lissa? The little pretty girl you used to run around with?" His uncle gave him a funny look.

"Yeah, we still friends. That's all. Just friends." Taj grinned, thinking his uncle was looking at him like that and thinking he and Lissa had something going on.

"Just be careful wit' who you put in your business," James warned.

"Aw, Unc', Lissa is cool. I trust her more than most niggas," Taj said before dapping his uncle up and going inside.

James sat looking at his hands pensively, before making a call.

***

The night of her abortion was the worst. She had very little pain, but psychologically she wasn't doing her best. Taj hung around until she basically put him out, she was tired of his prying, knowing eyes and of Zandra calling every ten minutes to see where he was.

He refused to leave until Jamila had gotten in the bed and was asleep, which didn't take long because she had worn herself out playing with him.

Getting in the bed, her body felt unnatural, as if it knew that she had gone against the laws of nature by getting rid of her baby. Tears wouldn't come, but neither would sleep. Every sound in her apartment was illuminated, from the hum of the refrigerator, the murmurings of her neighbors, to the cars passing by.

After tossing and turning, she finally drifted off to sleep, only to wake up soon. She sat straight up. Running into Jamila's room, she saw her sweet baby sleeping peacefully. She crawled in the bed and pulled Jamila close to snuggle with her, then tears flowed.

"Lord, please forgive me of my sins. My sins caused all of this to happen to me, but please Lord, don't let anything happen to my precious baby. I give all praise to you, Lord, for all your blessings. Just please keep my baby safe from seen and unseen dangers. Please forgive me of this sin. Amen."

The sea of hurt, disgrace and disappointments flowed freely, soaking her pillow. She uttered no sound; just letting the tears fall until she went to sleep.

Dark storm clouds rolled in the sky. The wind was fierce, whipping the tall grass around a woman with long hair that swept behind her, clarifying her brilliant eyes. It was her grandmother, a younger version and her eyes shone brightly, piercing Kalissa in fear. When her grams opened her mouth, there were no teeth, just a brilliant red, but her voice boomed in Kalissa's ears.

"As a child you learned not to trust, as a teen you learned to doubt yourself, now you will learn that your experiences will either give you power or break you. Turning all pain into empowerment is a gift, it's in you to use."

An incoming call woke Kalissa up. She shivered. "What the hell was that?" she murmured softly, while patting the bed for her phone. Jamila moved closer, radiating a sweet heat.

"Hello?"

"Come open the door."

Whew, I can't tell anybody about that crazy dream, she thought. Before getting out of the bed, a smile crossed her lips as she realized why her dad always said she reminded him of his mother. Their resemblance was clear in her dream. Softly padding to the front, she let Taj in.

"What's up?" she asked looking at him quizzically.

"Nothing, go get me some covers, man, I'm sleepy!"

"Taj?"

"Uh-uh, just get the covers and hush. I'm staying here to-night."

Walking to him timidly, she put her arms around his midsection and laid her head on his chest.

Taj wrapped her up in a hug, looking at the top of her head and realizing that for all her book sense and little street sense, she was still so innocent.

"Thank you for being my friend, Bro."

"That's forever. We'll be friends until we are old and gray, can't nothing come between us. Now go get me some cover!"

Watching her move to the back, he rearranged his dick in his pants, because the last thing she needed was to know that holding her close had turned him on. Instead of giving him the throw and leaving, she settled under it with him and talked his ears off long into the night.

C.D. Blue

CHAPTER 12

Zo pulled up at his uncle's home, eyeballing the Impala parked on the side of the street. He had been avoiding this meeting for as long as he could. But when his uncle threatened to come to his place, he knew he had to come. Ureka never cleaned up and he didn't want to hear Uncle James mouthing off about the mess. Plus he was running low on cash, since his bitch ass cousin had kicked him to the curb.

James opened the door, eyeballing Zo with a scowl. Ushering him in, he stopped him when Zo tried to walk towards the kitchen.

"Nah, nigga, bring yo' ass outside. I've been waiting on yo' for a couple of weeks, this ain't no lunch and learn."

"Damn, Unc', let a nigga get a snack or something! I'm starvin'."

With James being over six feet, he looked down in Zo's face. "I don't give a fuck. And if I ever have to call yo' ass more than once again, the only muthafuckin' thang you'll sell in the Gump is Happy Fuckin' Meals."

Zo nodded, finally seeing the man that so many feared in Montgomery. He followed him to the patio, where a dark-skinned dread head guy sat smoking a cigar.

"Zo, this is Rollo and you'll be working with him for now." James sat back in the plush lawn sofa.

Zo, who remained standing, looked from Rollo to James in anger. "Unc', I thought you was gonna let me run thangs on my own? I don't know this nigga."

James stopped midway from lighting his cigarette, his face showing his annoyance. Rollo just gave a half smile.

"Rollo, lemme holla at my nephew for a minute. If you go in the kitchen its some oxtails, rice and cabbage in there, help yourself," James said patiently.

Zo's mouth gaped in a scowl, as Rollo passed by him chuckling. He looked at his uncle. But before he could complain, James snatched his arm and threw him down on the chair.

"Looka here, yo' ass can't even git over here on time, so how the fuck you think I'ma let you run any damn thang? You gotta prove yaself, Zo, damn! You gonna run yo' mouth right into a job at Mickey D's!"

Zo watched his uncle talk with the long Newport jumping with every word, unlit. He was surprised the fire in his eyes hadn't lit that bitch.

Rubbing the little stubble on his chin, Zo nodded, "You right, Unc'. I 'preciate you putting me on and I apologize for coming at you sideways like that. I was just thinking—"

"That's why don't no damn body pay you to think," James cut him off. "And what the hell did you do to that pretty lil' girl? Tee's friend . . ."

Reclining back in his chair, Zo grimaced. "I didn't do shit to that hoe! Tee just mad she gave me the pussy instead of him."

James took a hard pull off his cigarette, staring out in his yard, sucking his teeth for what seemed like forever, but was actually only a few minutes.

"I want you to lissen to me real good, son. Rollo is a stone cold killa, period. So make sure you have his money on time and accounted for, don't dip into the product and don't even look at any damn woman that is in his presence. Do you understand?"

Not waiting for an answer, James continued, "Rollo will put you in the dirt, I guarantee you that. Tee ain't no killa and you his family. You ain't shit to Ro, but another nigga in the street."

"I hear ya," Zo said loudly, then muttered, "but I am too."

"Good, go in there and get Rollo, so we can talk about bizness. And yeah, you can fix you a plate, wit' yo' begging ass."

Once a plan was in place and the two men left, James walked in his den, where his sixty-five inch television played loudly, and sat heavily on the sofa. Deep down he knew he should have cut off Zo, because he was a loose cannon. But he was also family and somebody had to take his place whenever he gave it all up. It was up to him to get them ready.

With a heavy sigh he pulled the burner phone from his pocket and called his connect.

"Yeah, it's all taken care of," he said as soon as the man picked up.

Listening intently, he nodded, "Yeah, I'ma get them all together soon to give them the lay of the land. Huh?"

Listening again as he was questioned, his gut tightened.

"Nah, that's handled. It was just a minor disagreement that got out of control. I think Zo will be better off with Rollo anyway."

The deep voice droned on for a few more minutes before hanging up. The connect had a slight accent that was hard to detect. The man ran the entire state; no one knew who he was, his cronies were always sent. This fact, along with his gut, told him to keep the information about the fallout to himself.

Standing up and stretching, he felt as if his nephews would be the death of him, especially Zo. That lil' nigga didn't understand that the game was serious and there were only three ways to leave it. *Standing. Six feet under. Or in a steel cage.* His plan, however, was to leave it standing.

Taj wasn't a killa but he might need to learn to be if he planned on staying in the game. Maybe he could teach Taj other skills so that he could take his money and turn into a normal life. He looked at his hands, thinking of all the blood on them and the things he'd done that kept him awake some nights.

With legitimate businesses, the money wasn't exciting him anymore. He was tired of every other day seeing in the news these youngbloods connected to him dying in the streets. He was getting too old for this shit!

Hopefully, teaming Zo with Rollo wouldn't be the death of his foolish nephew.

C.D. Blue

CHAPTER 13

3 months later

"Love" by Keyshia Cole blared through the speakers of her new Honda Accord. It was slightly used but new to Kalissa and a gift from her dad. The sun beaming through the windshield matched her mood.

Down and out Lissa was gone! Her swag was back, with a vengeance! The incident had been cleared from her head, Zo hadn't bothered her again, her bank account was looking good, and her bills were paid. Waiting on the cars to pass so that she could pull into work, she saw Brian hanging out in the parking lot, standing by his blue Chevy Malibu.

"Hey, I thought you was coming in early?" he said to her as soon as her car door opened.

"I'm fifteen minutes early! That's enough time for you to get a kiss." She flirted shamelessly, tilting her head up to him.

Taking the bait, he kissed her shyly on the side of her mouth. This had been the game they had been playing for a couple of months. His old grumpy attitude had changed after her 'incident' made her calm down some. It took him a minute to ask for her number, but once he did, they had some long late night calls which then turned into a few dates. No sex yet, but they were official.

Giving him a once-over behind her shades, he didn't notice the slight nod of her head. Tall, around six-two, Brian had a light brown complexion and he wasn't muscular, but what her momma called big boned. Kind of country, but a real nice guy. He wasn't street, he worked hard and there was an innocence about him.

The most important thing was that he was safe. Calm, no drama, but he also didn't generate any butterflies or excitement. Just what she needed, so she kept telling herself. With all that against him, he still was better than the alternatives of the last niggas she'd dealt with.

"Before we go in, you want to go out tonight?" His shyness was sweet, boring but sweet.

"Yeah, if I can get a sitter we'll do it."

Taking a mental reminder that she needed a safe, regular guy didn't stop her body from tensing up. That was a part of her leftover trauma, thanks to Zo. Brian had never been any further in her apartment than the door; she met him outside if he picked her up or she just drove to the appointed destination.

Walking in together caused little stir in the restaurant, their co-workers had gotten used to seeing them together. Kalissa seemed to be the only who struggled with it.

During her shift, it was confirmed that her sister would keep Jamila. Guilt slipped through her because she worked so many hours, she always felt bad about taking more time away from her baby. This night was going to have to be worth it for that.

Of all days, the closer was late. Since Kalissa couldn't leave until night shift was fully staffed she was running behind. By the time she showered, put on her black jeans with a fitted vee-neck top, combed her hair and applied a little make-up, Brian was knocking on the door.

Overlooking that he looked like a farmer, she walked out without letting him in.

"Hey, I hope we aren't late for the movie," she said.

"It doesn't matter. I have the tickets already. You look so pretty,"

"Thanks," she murmured, grabbing his hand. "After the movie, let's get a room." Her apartment was her sanctuary and she wasn't ready for him to invade it.

Stopping in his tracks, his eyes lit up like a Christmas tree. "Why don't we skip the movie and just do that? Your daughter must be at home?"

"Umm-hmm, yep she is. I thought you said you had tickets already? That would be a waste of money."

"Shit, it will be worth it! Unless you really want to see the movie?" Always the nice guy, he waited for her answer.

"Nah, not really, "she answered truthfully. Because what she wanted to do was get the night over with and go to sleep.

Usually a slower, safer driver, Brian had his Malibu moving! This was obviously something he had been wanting, but hadn't had the nerve to speak up. Another check in the "this-isn't-going-to-work speech" that was formulating in her head for when it was needed. His dick would have to have a firecracker attached to it to keep that from happening.

Once in the room, she got cold feet. Just looking at his Timberland boots on the floor made her shake her head.

"Hey, what's wrong? Come here," he said patting on the spot next to him on the bed.

"Wait, I'ma go outside and smoke first. You know, calm my nerves," she smiled at him sweetly.

He made a face, because he knew she smoked and had voiced his displeasure about it numerous times. "Just do it in here, I don't want anybody to call the cops."

Widening her eyes, trying not to laugh, she knew this nigga was super excited. Kind of made her feel like a celebrity.

"I don't know why you smoke that stuff," he grumbled as she lit up.

She blocked out all sounds and sights, letting the weed take her where she needed to be. As soon as she stubbed it out, she felt his hands on her shoulders. Feeling so relaxed, it didn't bother her as much. Surprise lit her face when she turned and realized he was out of his clothes with his dick in her face. He wasn't getting any head, she wasn't that high. He led her to the bed and kissed her, putting his tongue in her mouth while his lips covered her face.

"You gonna take your clothes off?"

"Yeah, yeah, let's turn a little music on, is that okay?"

With his head bobbing, he was in bed with his dick in his hand, stroking it and watching her every move. Putting on Mariah Carey, it didn't matter what song, the kiss was obviously his foreplay. Usually being in the mood with music made her strip seductively out of her clothes, just naturally. Since being raped, she just didn't feel herself anymore; it never crossed her mind that her lack of natural attraction to Brian had anything to do with it. Instead she just felt damaged.

Expecting him to pounce on her, she relaxed as he cupped her face softly in his hands and kissed her. It was nice, but the extent of his foreplay.

His stroke was gentle, almost as if he was afraid that he would hurt her. Moving in time to the music that played, she moaned. She had to admit it to herself: some of it was real, but most was fake and the rest was from the blunt.

"Let me get on top before you come," she whispered in his ear.

Brian pulled out quickly and as they changed positions, he tried to kiss her.

"Not yet, just relax and feel me."

He closed his eyes, his face crunched up from her sliding up and down on his pole, and she couldn't help but smile at this scenario.

"Hey, look at me" she commanded, stopping and squeezing his head with her muscles.

"Agghh," he groaned loudly, his hands moving to her hips.

"Come on, open your eyes. I want you to look at me when you nut," she teased, moving slowly down his dick just a little.

Brian opened his eyes and stared at her with lust as she slammed down on his groin. Leaning forward, she licked his lips with her tongue, never breaking eye contact. His hands guided her hips and the more she leaned forward, the better he felt. Each time Brian tried to catch her tongue, she moved back ever so elusively. Five minutes later, he gripped her hips and she sensed his dick getting so hard it felt like a pipe.

Giving a stand-up performance, Kalissa arched her back and gripped his shoulders. Once she felt him vibrating inside of her, she leaned forward and sucked his neck almost like a vampire out for blood.

"Oh shit! Oh shit! Here it comes!" His deep voice resounded in the cheap hotel room.

After what seemed to last longer than the actual act, he stopped shaking and she looked at the dark red circle on his neck. Flopping down on his chest as if she was tired, his cologne tickled at her nose. It didn't smell as good as it had earlier. After carefully dislodging from his still hard dick, she rolled on her side, draping her leg over his.

"Damn, Kalissa, that was the icing on the cake." Brian chuckled. "You are full of surprises."

"What's that mean?" Propping her head on her hands Kalissa looked intently at him.

"You're just so different than I thought you would be when I first met you."

"That's because you were so busy being mean to me!" She laughed.

"I know I was I was attracted to you from the beginning, but I thought you was just one of them stuck up shallow women."

Placing her hand over her left breast, she looked at him in fake surprise. "Who? Me?"

Chuckling, he kissed her in the middle of her forehead. "Yep. But you not. I mean you ain't stuck up at all and definitely not shallow, nowhere." He glanced down. "You deep as hell. I was scared that your little ass wouldn't be able to take all of me."

Raising her eyebrows while looking at his shrinking member, she had to admit he was a nice size, but definitely not all he was making it out to be.

"Umm-hmm, that's what you get for judging a book by its cover." Rolling over, she flung her arm over her face. The bed shifted slightly as he moved closer.

"Kalissa? I was thinking, you know I'll probably get the kitchen manager job soon," he cleared his throat. "I was wondering if when I do if we can maybe move in together. You know . . . to a better apartment complex."

She had the initial, inbred instinct to run out of the room butt naked; instead, she took a deep breath.

"You really think you want to do that?"

"You don't have to look like you smell something," he said, laughing. "Yeah, I know you're what I want."

Back to the original reason they were together, he was safe. Safe, hardworking, and truly a nice guy. Suddenly she was daydreaming of not having to work so hard and much, maybe even go back to school and get a job with normal hours, holidays off and good benefits. Kalissa closed her eyes, picturing a nice apartment, her in an apron cooking cookies for her daughter and having a man come home to her every day.

"Kalissa? You there? Do you hear me?"

She opened her eyes and smiled into his earnest ones. "Yep, it sounds good to me."

CHAPTER 14

"Poppy!" Jamila screamed as soon as she saw her granddad.

Dew was still falling on the grass, the sun barely peeped out, but Kalissa and her daughter were up and about. Jamila was so excited about her Poppy coming to get her, she barely slept. Truth be told, Kalissa was excited too. A week of pure freedom, other than her job.

"Hey, little precious. Are you ready?" Lissa's dad, Henry, bent down slowly.

Admiring him from the door, it crossed her mind that he wasn't getting any younger. Even if he didn't believe it. There wasn't a speck of gray in his hair which he kept cut low, but his long beard was almost completely white. Standing a little under six feet, he was still slim and got around fairly well. Wearing khaki Dockers and a long sleeve button down azure shirt under a soft leather jacket, the only indication that he was wealthy was the large solitaire 3 carat pinky ring that shone so brightly it could be spotted a mile away.

"Daddy, you know I live in the hood, why you wearing that ring over here?"

"Aww, these youngins don't want none of this smoke. I promise you that," he laughed.

That was no lie, he was the toughest, meanest man she had ever known. The main reason she barely had any boyfriends growing up: everybody was scared of him. People always asked about his ethnicity, until he opened his mouth; he talked fast, but country as hell.

"Where's Grammy? She didn't come with you?" Kalissa asked as she packed Jamila's cup into the bag.

"Nope, you know your grandmother was still asleep. She worked herself up in a tizzy about this little baby coming. She was worn out."

"Umm-hmm, you just need to be careful out here in these streets by yourself, you aren't as young as you think," she murmured.

It was funny seeing her dad out by himself. He was one of five brothers; usually he had his brothers with him. As soon as Kalissa left home, her dad and his brothers bought close to one hundred acres in a small town called Towndesboro, built their houses, packed up, and left Montgomery. Since they all lived within a mile or two of each other, if you saw one you'd see another.

When Kalissa was small her dad always worked at least two jobs to take care of them. Then he won a pretty big lawsuit against one company and invested in property. He shared the wealth with his brothers.

"My hand still steady enough to fill a few of these nephews with lead, don't you worry about me." He looked at her strangely.

"The next time I come here, I'm taking you shopping, every time I see you, seems like you wearing the same thang."

"These are my work clothes! I work all the time, that's why I'm always wearing the same thang," she mocked him.

"Kalissa, you smart enough to be sitting behind a desk, I don't know why you insist on working at that restaurant. Oh, yes. I do. You too hard-headed to lissen to anyone."

An age-old argument, but as many times as he fussed about it, she would—as she did this time around— nod her head, agreeing with him.

Kissing her baby and rushing them out of the door so she wouldn't be late, the long awaited freedom felt funny. It felt so weird she was tempted to go get her baby when she got off.

Seeing Brian waiting for her with anticipation on his face changed those thoughts. He was beginning to grow on her, somewhat.

"Hey, I was wondering if you were going to show up. Did your baby make it off okay?" Without waiting for an answer he kissed her, like, a real kiss.

Drawing back because she wasn't one for public displays of affection, she noticed the hurt in his eyes.

"So, what do you want to do tonight?" he asked turning the tables.

"Umm, I'm not sure. I'll let you know later."

114

Close to the end of her shift, things changed as soon as she received a text from Taj.

Taj: we meeting up at Fefe's tonight

Lissa: who all coming?

Taj: Fam, jus bring yo' azz on

Lissa: bet, I'll be there

Plans had changed! Not only could Fefe cook her ass off, it was going to be so much fun, she just knew it. A little bit of guilt tapped her shoulder, but she shrugged it off. Jamila would be gone for a whole week, she'd get with Brian another day.

"Hey, what's up? You decided what you wanted to do tonight?"

As if by osmosis, this nigga appeared up front, behind her.

"Well, I was just about to come back there. My girlfriend just moved into a new apartment. Me and some of her other friends are going to help her fix it up. Umm, she's having a house warming party this weekend. So we just gonna have a girls' night. Can we get together another night?"

Disappointment was evident in his body language and he narrowed his eyes meanly.

"Damn, Kalissa! I thought we were going to spend some time?"

Since they were at work, she kept it professional. "And we will, but not tonight. I'm hanging out with my girls and that's that."

Pivoting on the ball of her feet, she tried to turn when he snatched her arm. When she gasped in surprise, his look changed and he moved his hand.

"I'm sorry Kalissa, I didn't mean to"

"Oh, hell nah! I can't believe you did that! Just get away from me," she hissed.

Still trying to apologize, he walked away with his shoulders slumped. It took all of her facial muscles not to crack a smile. That had worked out perfect, because now she had the perfect excuse for him not to hear from her tonight. It was party time!

***

"Hey, hey, I made it!" Kalissa singsang as she waltzed into Fefe's apartment. Lil' Wayne was rocking on the stereo, a long rectangular table was set up against the wall with wings, meatballs, chips a fruit tray on one side and bottles of liquor on the other end. Fefe knew how to set up and throw a get-together.

Cedric, Desi and Duke were at the food end of the table. Taj eased out of the kitchen as she walked into it. He gave her a once-over before they hugged.

"Look at you, showing off that ass! Girl, who you trying to catch? I thought you had a man." Fefe screamed after turning away from the stove to look at her friend.

Kalissa had worn a long sleeved multi colored, lacy, see-through top that flared over her hips which were covered by black form-fitting leggings and a pair of black Nine West pumps. When she looked at her body she saw a small bump of booty, not realizing that since her waist was so small, her butt was big for her frame.

"You never know where I might go when I leave here, hmmm, the night is young," she joked, walking up to the stove. "You talm about me, look at you, with your girls hanging out tonight."

Fefe had on a short sleeved gold macramé-looking top that was low-cut, too little, but not as little as the burgundy jeans that barely covered her ass. When she bent over, half of the crack of her ass showed. As much as she loved her friend, all clothes were not meant for everyone to wear.

Taj returned to the kitchen, handing her a white plastic cup which burned her nose when she sniffed it.

"Now you know I don't really drink and even if I did you still can't beat me at Whist. I'm going to the smoking side!"

"Oh, I'ma beat your ass tonight, no doubt. I brought my secret weapon." Taj laughed as she looked around the room.

"I hope you ain't talking about Cet, 'cuz I used to beat him daily in Study Hall," she whispered loudly.

"I hear ya', woman. I've gotten better since then."

Everyone laughed. She fixed a plate and halfway through the first hand, there was a loud knock.

116

"I got it!" Fefe yelled since she wasn't playing.

Desi, who lied obviously and said he could play, had just cut her Queen. Feeling tipsy, Kalissa stood up, "Mane, you got one mo' time to cut me! I'm yo' patna, dammit!"

Card games turned her into a completely different person, she was super competitive, serious and a damn good player.

"My bad, I forgot you played the Queen," Desi said slowly, hitting his blunt.

Taj hung off his chair, laughing.

"Whoa, you might need a new potna," that came from a very deep voice.

Kalissa looked up into the sexiest pair of light brown eyes she'd never thought she'd ever see again. Nigel gave her a sneaky smile.

"Well, hey, lil' mama, I thought you was a figment of my imagination."

He kept his eyes on her while he pulled off his large jacket, showing his oversized blue Seattle Seahawks jersey and baggy blue jeans. His hair had grown out since she last saw him, it was curly on top, faded on the sides, and he was looking fine as hell.

"Aye, cuz, you gonna introduce me or what?" his homeboy inquired.

"My bad. Kalissa, this is my cuz Rod. Rod, this is Kalissa Never Calls."

Rod stepped forward while everyone laughed. Rod was the direct opposite of Nigel. Shorter, buffed-chested, serious looking with his hair cut in a mohawk dyed auburn on the top. Kalissa shook his hand while she blushed.

The men carried the cases of beer they brought, into the kitchen, and they resumed their game, which Kalissa and Desi lost.

"It's time for someone to get up!" Duke came from out of nowhere to declare.

"Come on, Desi, we loss."

"I'm gonna play with my brother, whatchu talm 'bout?"

Busy talking shit, Desi wasn't quick enough when Kalissa stomped over shoeless, snatched his blunt and scampered to the sofa. Fefe stood at the table with the other two men showing them where everything was. While they were occupied, Kalissa kept glancing at Nigel through the haze of smoke. Keeping her cool façade, she didn't flinch when he sat right beside her.

"So, lil' baby, what you been up to?" His voice didn't match his look, it was so deep and gruff, but she liked it.

"Which one am I? Lil' mama or lil' baby?" she asked smartly, flipping her hair back over her shoulder.

"You both of 'em to me. How 'bout that?"

That broke the ice, the next thing she knew they were talking, laughing, she was taking his plate to the trash and bringing back Heinekens. Whatever cologne he was wearing was tickling her panties! Somewhere in their conversation she revealed that she was seeing someone.

"He must have been working on you the first time we met." He gave her that devilish smile.

"Umm, nah, we're pretty recent, I was just getting over a long relationship when I met you," she batted her eyelashes. "I lost your number, that's why I didn't call, but you musta lost mine too."

"What kinda nigga let a pretty lil' mama out by herself early? He must not know about me," Nigel said before getting up.

"Know what about you?"

"Fe! Where's that ole school CD I gave you?"

Either she was tipsy or he was just loud. Fefe told him where to look on the stand that held her Bose stereo.

"Don't do it to her, my nigga," Rod, who had been quiet, said with a grin.

Usher's "Nice and Slow" started playing through the speakers. Nigel grinned at her, started grinding his hips to the music and then began singing while looking at her. He sounded so good she got caught up in the moment.

When he held out his hand she was putty, all she could do was stand and go to him. Their grinding was synchronized and hypnotic, seemingly choreographed. Placing his hands expertly on her hips, he led her, while she twisted her hips against his feeling his erection.

Everyone in the room was entranced by the scene. The next tune by Joe, "All the Things (Your Man Won't Do)" came on and Nigel nudged her away from him slightly when he belted out the lyrics. Hands above her head, eyes closed with her head back, she lost herself in the music, winding her hips seductively to the beat. Oblivious to how her sensuality had captured every man in the room.

"Lawd, I hope she don't start stripping," Taj laughed drunkenly as he watched.

"If she does we will not stop her, y'all hear?" Cedric watched the scene, captivated yet jealous at the same time.

"Humph," Fefe said, wringing her dish towel as she stood at the entrance of the kitchen watching.

Pulling her to him, Nigel continued singing, then stopped to lean down to kiss her. She was lost in her feelings. Funnily enough, it seemed as if everyone had disappeared and they were the only ones in the room. His lips were soft, but demanding, causing her to soak her panties and taking her breath away. Breaking away, he licked down her neck, still singing softly about all he could do. And she wanted him to, right then and there.

Fighting the inexplicable urge to take her clothes off, she was glad and sad at the same time when the song ended. Kissing her lightly on her cheek, he winked at her.

Not sure if it was the weed, the beer, or the heavy sexual tension, but she stood on the sofa to make an announcement.

"Next get-together is at my place! Tomorrow. Wait, not tomorrow, but Wednesday when I'm off. Everybody's invited and brang your own damn bottles!"

Raising his eyebrows, Nigel helped her off the sofa and she gathered her shoes, knowing that if she didn't leave right then she could not be held accountable for any of her actions.

"Where you going?" Nigel asked, looking at her crazy.

"Home, I've got work, early in the morning."

"Nah, you ain't driving home by yourself," his voice boomed.

Interest sparked in her eyes, then the thought of Zo's stanking ass invaded her thoughts. "Uhh, I'll be alright, thanks. It's not far."

"Nah, I'll drive you, and Rod can follow us. Perfectly innocent, I promise." He held his hands up, his eyes undressing her.

"Well . . ."

"Where yo' keys?" he demanded.

Fefe and Taj looked at them in amusement as they left, Lissa promising Taj—before he let her out the door—she would call him as soon as she made it home.

They made it to her house quicker than she had ever driven there; Nigel drove like a bat out of hell! Breathing a sigh of relief when they pulled into the parking lot, she held her hand out for her keys.

"Thanks, I really appreciate it."

"You live upstairs or down?" Nigel asked, while running his finger up her thigh.

"Umm, upstairs," she murmured because once again she was caught up in a sexual fog.

"Do I need to carry you up?" His finger moved to the inside of her thigh tracing circles or octagons, or something.

"Nah, I'm good. Whatever high I had . . . I lost with your driving." She laughed nervously.

"There's somethin' about you, lil' mama, and I'm gonna find out what it is. I don't give a fuck about your boyfriend."

Putting her lips together she looked at him, ignoring his light brown eyes shining through the darkness.

"You trying to run game on me?"

Rubbing the tip of his nose with the back of his hand, he chuckled. "I was . . . earlier, but not now. I'm serious."

"Don't make me show you how it's—" He cut her off with a kiss. Not just a regular kiss, but one that sent tingles down her pussy.

Tweaking her titties with his hand, she reached for his dick, feeling the outline of the head through his jeans. Moaning in his mouth, they were stopped by Rod blowing his horn.

"Damn!" he breathed heavily, shaking his head.

Gathering herself, she opened her door, frustrated and tempted to ask him upstairs. Fuck a first night rule!

Shaking her head, she thanked him again and headed up the sidewalk.

"Kalissa!"

Looking back, he was leaning against her driver's door, motioning for her to come to him. Kalissa walked slowly to him, mainly because of her heels, and he circled her waist with both of his hands, almost intertwining them when she stood in front of him. Beginning with her nose, then her lips and working his way to her neck, he kissed her again. It felt as if her juices were dripping down her leg and she was so turned on that her pussy was in pain.

"We ain't finished, I'll be seeing you soon."

One more kiss sealed her fate. It finally hit her that she hadn't had to play-act and her body was responding naturally. She knew then that she was in trouble!

Neither of them noticed the blue Malibu tucked away in the far corner of the parking lot.

C.D. Blue

CHAPTER 15

"Mane, what you know about this Niger homes?" Cet, Taj and Desi were hanging outside of Cedric's momma house.

"Who the hell is Niger, chief?" Taj frowned while Desi fell out laughing.

"The nigga from last night with Lissa! Who is that nigga? I don't remember him from school."

"Oh, he didn't go to school wit' us. He's cool. I know Rod, his cousin. They straight." Taj waved at some young women passing by slowly in a car.

"Humph, I can't believe we was so fucked up that we let him take her home. That shit wasn't right." Cedric mumbled the last part.

"It was cool, she called me when she made it in by herself. You know Lissa don't really fool around with niggas in the game too tough. Not like that."

"I shole couldn't tell last night," Desi put in his two cents' worth.

Cedric pulled a Newport out of the box, lit it, and paced on the porch. "Then this nigga had the nerve to be sanging and shit! Who the fuck does that?"

"It looked like it worked." Desi was still laughing.

Stopping in mid pace, Cedric narrowed his eyes. "Keep running yo' fuckin' mouth, you gonna be picking yo' teeth up off my momma's porch."

The plastic lawn chair shook with Desi's laughter, even as he tried to stifle it.

"Man, Lissa is seeing some lame. She's cool. The real question is when you moving out yo' momma's house? Damn! I know you make enough money. I'm tired of standing outside."

Unable to hold it back, the chair—with Desi in it—fell sideways as he laughed harder. Cedric glowered at both of the men.

"I'm saving up for a house. Y'all know I got my lawn business, so I can have a way to show my income. I ain't trying to live in no apartment. Lissa will look at me then. White picket fence, backyard, oh yeah, come to daddy."

Dancing around the front yard, he croaked out a couple of bars of some song they couldn't decipher. Only he knew what he was trying to sing.

"Cet! Cet!" Taj tried to get his attention.

"What up?"

"Give it up, that shit won't work."

Feigning sadness, Cet responded, "You right, if they get together they won't eva break up! As soon as she gets mad that nigga gonna sang and dance to make up."

Taj laughed then changed the subject. "You know Zo working with Rollo now. Unc' set it up. His ass won't even speak to me when I see him."

Cedric's eyes widened. "Rollo? That crazy ass nigga? You unc' must want Zo dead. Rollo don't play about shit, I ain't never seen that nigga smile a day in his life. He was mad in elementary school."

"I don't remember him from school. Unc' must know something for him to have paired Zo with Rollo. But this nigga still riding in that Altima! And the muffler still jacked up." Taj shook his head.

"'Member, I didn't meet y'all until middle school. We had moved by then and I'm not sure where he went to high school, shid, or if he even went. All I know is he put a nigga eye out for saying something sideways to one of his baby mommas."

"Who?" Taj looked interested.

"You know one-eyed Shane. That's what happened to that nigga. All I say is, I'm glad I'm wit' you. Ain't no fucking way I would want to work for Rollo. Shid, I'd go work at the chicken factory befo' I do that."

Although he would never admit it to anyone, the distance between him and Zo bothered him. As bad as Zo got on his nerves, they were like brothers and the disconnect was felt. Part of him wanted to warn his cousin about what Cedric said. As much as he felt like they were siblings, he knew his uncle thought of both of them as sons. Trusting his uncle's judgment was the best he could do.

Puffing his chest out as he looked in the driveway, he was proud of his crew. Cedric had bought a new Ford Explorer, fitted with rims and tint. Desi had gotten a Grand Prix that he was slowly fixing up, even Duke was riding in a Maxima. Dripping with designer fashions, their swag was official. Whatever Zo wanted to be mad about was on him. Things had looked up ever since he left, so Taj was glad he was gone.

***

The end of her shift couldn't come quick enough! It started good, except the niggling feeling that she should feel guilty. Brian had called her nineteen times last night and left almost as many voicemails and texts. Disregarding her lack of feelings due to not having to face him, since he was off, her day was going fine. Mid shift, she felt as if she had been hit by a truck. All she wanted was her bed.

"Hey, you gonna stay for dinner with me tonight? I think we're gonna be slow," her relief said shortly after arriving.

It was a ritual they usually did on the slow nights.

"Nah, I have a headache. Matter of fact, I'ma take off early, if it's all right with you?"

"Sure, I guess. You do look tired."

Struggling to control her facial expression, because she hated bitches always telling folks how they look. *Hoe, I asked you if I could leave, not how I look!* Instead of voicing her true feelings, she nodded and clocked out.

Brian began calling her as soon as she got in the car. She ignored it because it would be best to talk to him after she got some rest. There was a certainty that she would feel guilty by then.

Once Kalissa made it home, she showered, threw on some pink Victoria Secret sweatpants with a magenta wife beater and called her baby. She put her hair in one braid, jumped on the couch with a Sherpa throw and turned the television on.

Before long, there was a loud incessant knocking on her door. Wiping the slob off her cheek, she got up a little timidly and a little angry, thinking it was Brian.

It was Nigel!

"What happened to calling first?" Hiding her excitement, she propped her hip against the door.

"Check your phone. I called a few times and was a little worried, so I stopped by," he said gruffly.

"Oh. I was asleep. Last night and work wore me down, so . . ."

"So, let me in. I'm tired too." He stuck one foot in the door.

Kalissa opened the door with a laugh. He looked around, nodding slightly in approval. Thankfully, she had updated her furniture when she started making more money.

"Damn, baby, you sexy even when you to' the fuck up."

Frowning at his sideways compliment, she looked him over. Nigel threw his jacket on the chair, flexing in his deep purple jeans with the purple and white striped button down and matching Nike's. Diggin' his style, but not letting it show, she held back a compliment.

"I appreciate you checking on me, but I'm seriously tired." She swept her hand towards the sofa. "As you can see, I was sleeping."

"Lil' mama, I just wanna sit with you for a lil' while. Is that alright?"

With a small smack of her lips, she murmured, "I guess."

She went back to her spot on the sofa, but was in for a shock when he got on the other end and under the throw too. Shaking her head, she laughed and snuggled back under the warmth of the cover.

Obviously, his closeness made her comatose! Feeling her leg shake, it took her minute to realize where she was and what was going on.

"Lil' mama, someone knocking on your door," Nigel said, his voice full of sleep.

For the Love of a Boss

The lull of staying asleep was so tempting, but then she heard the banging. *That would surely get a complaint from her neighbors*, she thought. She looked through the peephole: it was Brian!

That woke her up quick! With another glance out and a look back at Nigel, she felt her heart pick up its pace, almost coming out of her chest. Wiping her hands across her clothes to straighten them, she cracked the door open and slipped out.

The cold air stung her all over, making her instinctively cringe. Brian looked at the closed door as if it had insulted him.

"Hey."

"Kalissa, why haven't you answered or returned my calls?" His face was a mix of worry and anger.

Once again that little voice failed her!

"I was going to call you after I woke up. I didn't feel like talking," she answered slowly.

"Hold up. So you think it's cool to just ignore me for two days?"

Hugging herself to ward off the cold, she just shrugged.

"Look, Brian, I didn't ignore you. We had an argument and both of us needed to cool off. I'm tired. I'll call you when I wake up. It's cold out here," she said.

"I'll come in."

"Noo, not tonight. Like I said, I'm tired."

His face mottled in anger as he slammed his fist on the door right above her head!

"I thought we were—"

"What's up? Why the fuck is you banging on dis door?"

As soon as she heard Nigel's voice and felt the heat from her apartment, she looked down at her feet, clueless as to what to say. When she finally looked up she wished she hadn't, Brian's expression went from shock to hurt—then anger—in a matter of seconds. Turning her head to avoid his hurt, she missed his hand reaching out for her. He wasn't quicker than Nigel.

He grabbed her waist and pushed her behind him, shielding her.

"Nah, you ain't 'bout to do that, not tonight."

"Nigga, you ain't got nothing to do this. Move out my way."

"Who da fuck you talking to? *This* ain't what you want," Nigel narrowed his eyes and bit his bottom lip while moving his shirt back to flash the nine millimeter tucked in his pants.

Brian looked from Nigel to Kalissa, who all of sudden had no little or big voice; she was shocked into silence.

"We'll talk later, Kalissa. For real." He gave that parting shot before he ambled down the steps.

Nigel pulled the door shut and locked it. He wrapped his arms around Lissa, making her feel comfortable and safe in his warmth.

"You good lil' baby?" He kissed her face.

"Umm." That sexual tension had a hold on her again. From his cologne, his body heat and hard body. That ended when her hip hit hard steel.

Kalissa pushed him away and slapped his shoulder. "Why did you bring that gun in here?"

Nigel rubbed his face and gave her a strange look. "Ain't no nigga gone ever catch me slipping, that's how muthafuckas get killed."

He put the 9 on the coffee table, leaned back on the sofa and opened his arms. Rolling her eyes, it amazed her how he switched from Bruce Lee mode to being Marvin Gaye in a matter of seconds. She felt his eyes boring into her thin shirt and she knew her nipples were on display from the cold air.

That look, combined with the sweet comfort she found in his arms, led her back to the couch. Lying on top of him, she soaked in his heat.

"I'ma ask you again, you good?" His breath was in her hair.

Nodding into his neck, she ran her tongue on the side of it, tasting a mixture of salt and cologne.

"Umm, don't start nothing you can't finish." His voice was hoarse with lust.

She nibbled on his jawbone and chin, working her way up to his lips. His hands were everywhere, but his mouth covered hers as she playfully alternated between biting and sucking his lower lip.

128

For the Love of a Boss

What sounded like a growl came from her throat; before she knew what happened, she was on her back. The wife beater disappeared as his teeth grabbed the straps, then he branded her upper body with his hot tongue.

The heat that coursed through her was so strong and unlike anything she'd ever experienced before; it frightened her.

"Wait a minute." This was a whisper, her vocals cords had been burned and rendered weak in that heat.

Nigel stood up, never taking his eyes off her, as he removed his shirt—then his pants. Stroking his long, curvy dick that stuck out of his boxers, her hands moved on their own to take off her sweats.

Lapping the juices off her thighs with his tongue, when his brown eyes met her face, she lost it.

"I need you to fuck me right now!"

His hardness entered her wetness with a force that made her legs wrap around his back as her feet dug into him, pushing him deeper and deeper. When he hit the spot, it felt like an orchestra had come into her apartment playing sweet music, she heard it!

"Damn, yo' pussy so good, hot and fucking wet," he grunted over and over.

Each stroke made her hips jump higher to get all of his dick as deep into her as possible.

"Aw shit! Yo' dick feels good," she whimpered, licking her juices off his lips. When he ran his finger across her slit, she needed something in her mouth.

"Let me suck my pussy off your finger, baby," she begged.

He obliged, still hammering her, but once her lips wrapped around his finger she felt him get harder.

"Fuck, I'm about to come, lil' mama," he said in her ear.

Kalissa felt every spurt hitting deep inside her and her pussy clenched all the way around his dick, squeezing every drop.

Shell-shocked, they both lay there, breathing heavily, lost in the aftermath. He gave her that devilish grin, picked her up, and took her to the bedroom—for round two and three.

They spent the next two days together. Talking, laughing, sexing a lot and just hanging out. As many things as they had in common, there were just as many differences. Both had been left by their moms, but while Kalissa had been sheltered and secured by her dad's money and brothers, Nigel had been shuffled around a lot between his grandmother and aunt.

Similarly, they each had a child by their high school sweetheart; he had a son who was a year younger than Jamila. One stark difference was that underneath that tough guy façade, he had a big heart and a sensitive soul. Kalissa was just goofy and wore no façade.

The best part was how comfortable they were with each other. It seemed as if the stars had aligned just right and in their favor.

CHAPTER 16

Sunlight peeped through the blinds showing a flurry of dust floating around. Zo sat in the darkened room. He heard the scuttle of paper and looked at the nightstand to see two roaches fighting over a crust of bread.

Plap! He slapped his hand down, killing both of them in one swoop. Wiping his hands on his pants, he scowled into the silence. Closing his eyes, he tried to get back to sleep.

The screams of his baby shook him; his anger awoke. Seeing Taj the other day flaunting his money through his car and clothes along with that midget ass freak Cedric made his blood boil. Rollo crazy ass was so thorough; he had to buy his own blow. That nigga checked everything. His uncle pissed him off 'cuz he was the one who put him with that fool.

It was time for him to shine and run some shit. He was sick and tired of working for these niggas. When his phone rang, he glowered; it was Rollo.

"What it do?"

"Meet me outside in ten."

"Bet," Zo said to the air, because Rollo had hung up.

Before he could make it to the bathroom, Ureka came in sporting the black eye he gave her the other day.

"Where you going?"

"Why? Don't be asking me no stupid shit!"

"Zo, I need you to watch Lil' Man, I don't ever get a break and you don't ever spend no time with him." She pouted.

"Where the fuck you think you going looking like that? Move out my way, I got some business to handle," he growled, pushing her out of the way.

"Oww!" she yelled.

After giving it some thought, he reached in his pocket and threw the keys at her. "Here. You can drive my car, just take the lil' fucka with you."

Brushing his teeth and finding a stiff washcloth on the towel rack, he wiped his face. As he moved to the front he heard the beep of Rollo's horn.

The sun reflecting off the metallic bronze Impala didn't improve Zo's mood. Neither did seeing Rollo with his dreads piled on top of his head to showcase the huge diamond in his ear and wearing his Gucci shades. At least he was dressed down in a plain red tee shirt with faded black jeans.

"Nigga, I told ya ass to be outside," Rollo huffed with anger.

"Ole girl had some issues and held me up."

Rollo glanced at him, "Who running Adeline St.?"

He had to think fast 'cuz he knew Rollo was impatient as hell when he asked a question. "Oh, that Lil' Red, he running that shit!" Zo grinned proudly.

"Call that nigga up and tell him we 'bout to ride out," Rollo smiled.

Zo made the call and directed Rollo where to pick him up. Bopping his head to the music, he smiled thinking how his day had gotten better. Lil' Red was slinging hard and since Zo brought him in, this might be a step up the ladder and more money for him. That showed him that Taj didn't know what he was doing for kicking the youngin' out for one mistake. His time was coming!

They made it to Lil' Red's spot in record time. Lil' Red got in the backseat, a slight attitude on his face. "What up?"

"Jus' wanna talk to ya, lil' nigga, that's all," Rollo said, pulling off.

They rode in silence, all three men bopping along to the beat of Lil' Wayne.

Lil' Red broke the silence, "I hope this shit is important. It's early as hell."

Zo threw him a warning glance, but Rollo just laughed. "The early bird catch the worm, didn't yo' momma tell that?"

"My momma ain't told me nothing," Lil' Red said insolently.

"Well it ain't my fault yo' momma ain't teach you shit."

Lil' Red laughed but Zo started feeling funny from Rollo's tone. Glancing over at him, Rollo looked at him and smiled, so Zo thought it was just his imagination.

They rode to the back end of downtown, the part people didn't talk about since they had revitalized the area. It was full of dilapidated, deserted warehouses and barren land from where they had demolished the projects that used to be there.

Rollo pulled up to a warehouse that still had most of the windows. He turned the car off right there

"Y'all get out, I wanna show you something."

Getting out, Zo once again got a funny feeling. Lil' Red was dragging his feet but finally came and stood with other two men.

"Lil' nigga, did you get paid last night?" Rollo asked.

"Yeah, I got paid."

Nodding, Rollo looked at Lil' Red above his shades. "You got a lil' extra too, didn't you?"

That bad attitude came back out of Lil' Red. "Man, it was just a hunnid, that's all." He crossed his arms and glared at Rollo.

Whipping out his 357 Magnum, Rollo pointed it at Lil' Red. "It was just whose hunnid?"

Lil' Red's eyes got big, but he held onto his attitude.

"Wait a minute, man!" Zo appeased to Rollo, raising his hands.

Piercing Zo with his eyes for a second, Rollo said calmly, "Word? So, you wanna take this nigga bullet?"

Putting his hands down, he rolled his eyes up and stepped back.

"One mo' 'gin, lil' nigga. It was just whose hunnid?"

Still insolent, Lil Red answered, "I guess yours, nigga!"

With one crack, Lil' Red's brains flew out the back of his head; in slow motion his knees bent awkwardly as he fell to the ground. Rollo walked over to him and rambled through his pockets, taking all the cash out and stuffing it in his own.

"Nigga talm 'bout he guess, he knew that hunnid didn't belong to him." Rollo put his gun back in his pants. "Let's ride, nigga."

Still in shock at what he'd just witnessed, Zo made it slowly to the passenger seat.

"Mane, why you do that shit! He was just a kid!"

Rollo scratched his eyebrow, "If he was just a kid, his ass should have been at home doing kid thangs."

"His mom on that stuff, yo' know! He was just trying to survive. He didn't mean no harm. He woulda gave it back, damn!"

Rollo paused with his hand on the gearshift. "Nigga don't neva question me. That lil' dude did you a favor 'cuz that was your bullet. Let another muthafuckin' dime of mine come up missing from your crew. You next, ya heard?"

Shook, Zo could only nod and say, "Yeah, I hear ya."

***

Feeling pinpricks as though little knives were in her back, Kalissa knew it was Brian staring her down at her as she stood on the server line going over the new promotion. She was too tired and sore to care! It was a good sore because she'd just experienced the best two off days of her life! Moving away from the line, she smiled thinking about Nigel; he hadn't left her side since the night he showed up at her door. Her secret smile grew larger until she saw Brian glaring at her from the kitchen. Trying to look contrite but failing miserably, she just moved out of his line of sight. Kalissa knew she was wrong but justified it by telling herself it wasn't as if they had been in love. It was obvious that she wasn't ready for a live-in situation, still a few oats to sow.

"I see you got some rest! Girl, you are glowing!" her relief laughed when she walked up to Kalissa.

"Yeah, I did. It was much needed," she giggled.

"Umm-hmm, that looks like a I-just-got-fucked glow, if you ask me," the woman egged her on.

"Girl, I wish," Kalissa murmured. No one would ever catch her talking under a nigga nuts. She'd learned that lesson early on. Bitches would get all the tea then try to fuck to your nigga to see if they could get the same glow!

Once her shift was over, she tried to sneak to the back to clock out. Brian caught her as soon as she put her number in.

"You know we need to talk," Brian said, his lips close to her ear.

Jumping back because he frightened her, she gave a small smile and a nod. "Look, Brian, I'm sorry how things went down."

"That's it? You sorry?" He raised his voice.

Looking around nervously, Kalissa caught a few people glancing over at them.

"Uh, let's not put on a show for everybody, okay?"

"Okay, you right. Let's go outside," Brian said quietly.

Feeling pressured, Lissa looked around again, but seeing no way out, since she had to go outside to her car, she grabbed her jacket and followed him out the back.

"You could have just told me, Lissa," Clearly hurting, Brian's tone was low.

Feeling bad, she tried to explain, "There wasn't anything to tell. I didn't plan it, and it wasn't what you were thinking, anyway."

"It wasn't planned? You ignore me for two days then when I come over, you got another nigga at your place? How was that not planned?"

Unlocking her car, she sighed, tired of the conversation. "You were stressing me about going to my girlfriend's house, I don't need nobody checking me like that!"

Making an ugly face, his tone changed. "Here I am, trying to make a future with you and you straight playing games! You are just like I thought you were at first."

That last statement hit her wrong and Kalissa's mouth took over. "Nigga I didn't ask you to do shit! And I don't play games! I tole yo' ass I liked you and I do, I ain't never said I loved you! You tripping 'cuz I went out and there was a friend at my house when you stopped by unexpected? Well then, next time call before you come."

His mouth turned in an angry grimace. "It won't be a next time, I'm done with you. You just pretty wrapping paper, ain't shit to your ass for real."

"Okay, that's fine, whatever." Flipping her hand out, she got in her car.

CHAPTER 17

3 weeks later

The club was lit! People were filing in, some dressed to impress; others were simply dressed. The Flight was showcasing a local rap group in Montgomery and there had been so much buzz about it. Everybody showed up.

Nigel and Kalissa walked in as though they were royalty. The DJ played "Wait (The Whisper Song)" Nigel danced, creating a walkway, and Kalissa followed suit, holding his hand.

Nigel and Kalissa didn't half step; they were the best-looking couple there. Nigel had on a brown casual Fendi jacket and slacks with a gold tee shirt, looking handsome, with Kalissa on his arm. She wore a gold sequined dress that barely covered her little ass. Her hair hung down her back. She smiled 'cause the hoes were hating and the men were panting. Just the way she liked it.

"You want something to drink?" Nigel was close by.

From the moment they got out of the car, he kept her in his grip. This was their first time out clubbing. As fine as he looked, she was amenable to his charms. Turning to look into his brown eyes, she wanted to fuck him right there! This man had her dickmatized and she was not ashamed to admit it.

"Yeah, get me a beer."

"Naw, baby. You can drink beer at home. Out here you need some liquor. I'll get you something after I find us a table. I see I need to put you in a corner somewhere before I have to bust one of these niggas upside the head, for looking too hard."

A voice in the back of Kalissa's head wondered how the hell he thought he could tell her what to drink but she giggled aloud. "In Da Club" by 50 Cent was blaring through the speakers as Nigel led her dancing to the back of the club, stopping every five seconds to speak to someone. His cousin, Rod, trailed behind them, quiet as usual.

Once they sat down, Nigel headed to the bar, leaving her and Rod alone. Of all his friends and family, Rod was the only one she could tolerate. He was about his business and had sense. The rest of them just seemed to be bum ass niggas.

With a swift glance around, she saw big ballers, little ballers, small change, and a few bums. She could tell who was balling 'cause they had the most thirsty hoes hanging around. One dark-skinned guy who looked slightly familiar lifted his drink in the air to her. Wearing a ton of gold around his neck, arm and on his fingers, she knew he was a big baller! The woman with him looked in Kalissa's direction and scowled. Kalissa stared back with her head cocked to the side, never wavering.

"Who you mean mugging?" Nigel laughed as he approached with the drinks.

"Nobody. What you bring me?" Her scowl immediately turned into a smile.

"Some Henny, 'cause when we get back to your place I'ma make you cluck," Nigel said, before he leaned over and licked her face.

Blushing she rolled her eyes.

"I see yo' boy is here, too," Nigel said over the music.

"Who?"

He grimaced as he took a swig of his drink. She took one swallow of her own drink, the Hennessy burning her throat. The only person she regarded as 'her boy' was Taj; she knew he wasn't at the club. Nigel didn't answer, so she bobbed her head to the music.

"Hey! What up?" A woman with a red weave and blue contacts slid in Nigel's face.

"What up? Do I know you?" He waved her off.

"Oh, so it's like that? Humph, I see," she shot back, looking at Kalissa.

A tingly feeling started moving up Kalissa's spine as she saw the fake bitch was still only a few feet away from their table, throwing glances at them.

"I'm going to the restroom." She grabbed her clutch purse off the table.

"Don't make me come looking for you." Nigel grabbed her hand.

"Nah, what you need to do is get that shit over there straight," Kalissa said, snatching her hand back, looking over towards the wall.

Nigel looked at the girl and shrugged.

Kalissa followed the hand written signs signifying 'Emergency Exit/Restrooms' to the back of the club. Thankfully, there wasn't a line. It took three tries to find a halfway decent stall. The first one had pee and bloodstains on the seat; in the second one, somebody had taken a shit and didn't flush. The third was decent but smelled like piss.

Halfway squatting and half standing over the toilet, still mad about that disrespectful bitch, she positioned herself so that her pee wouldn't hit the floor. After wiping, she remembered she had half a joint in her purse. It took three deep pulls before she felt the tingling sensation go away. Satisfied, she walked out, washed her hands, feeling good.

The club's mirror wasn't very clean; she had to move her head from side to side to find a clear spot. She ran her hands through her hair, freshened up her lip gloss before smacking her lips together.

"Yep, you got it, bitch." She smiled at her reflection.

Her phone rang as soon as she pushed the door open. Fumbling around for it, as soon as she hit the green button to answer, she was slammed against the wall!

"So, you thought you was going play me, bitch?"

"What?" Kalissa was so surprised she didn't know what to say as she looked into the angry brown eyes of her assailant.

Her abuser led her to the exit, roughly pulling her arm. She tried to stop, but lost one of her shoes, scraping her foot as he dragged her outside.

"Let go of me!" she managed to yell, before he grabbed her around the neck and slung her against the building.

"You must have thought I was a fuckboy, huh? That's what you thought?"

His spittle slapped her face as she clawed at his hands, trying to break free. She felt the blood rushing to her head and tears swam in her eyes. Thoughts of her beautiful daughter flashed through her mind as his grip tightened more and more.

The next thing she knew she was on her knees gasping for air. Nigel appeared in a flash, dragged her assailant off her, and landed an uppercut in his jaw. Her attacker roared as he bum-rushed Nigel and slammed him into the dumpster, then delivered a hook to his side and a cross to his cheek. Gagging and coughing, Kalissa rose, trying to help, but heard the screech of tires.

Pop! Pop!

Rod shot through his open window and one bullet hit the guy in his shoulder.

"Oww!" the dude howled as he went down.

With her big toe throbbing, the rest of her foot burning, Kalissa hobbled over to Nigel to make sure he was alright as Rod got out of the car.

"Lissa, help me," her attacker croaked, with his hand stretched out.

Unsure of how to react, she looked at Nigel and Rod.

"Okay, I'll call . . ."

Pop! Pop! Pop!

Her eyes bulged as Rod put three bullets in her attacker's chest. Standing stock-still, she couldn't move. The man's breath turned ragged before his eyes seemingly fixed on her!

"Come on! We gotta go!" Nigel yelled, pushing her to the car.

Kalissa snatched her arm away. She clapped her hand over her mouth, hypnotized by the blackish blood seeping from under the guy. The blackness of the blood, as it trickled across the ground, made her feel the bullets must have wrecked untold havoc on the guy's system. Nigel yelled at her. She backed away, her eyes still glued to the blood. The building scraped her back as she bumped into it. Still in shock, she managed to retrieve her shoe. Hopping, her face contorted in agony, she made it to the car, and they peeled out of the parking lot.

They made it a safe distance from the club. Lissa was in the back seat holding her knees, rocking back and forth.

"Why did you kill him? Why did you have to kill him?" she screamed over and over.

Nigel looked back at her. "Calm down, Lissa."

Her throat burned partly from screaming, the other part from being strangled nearly to death, but that didn't stop her from yelling at Nigel.

"Don't fucking tell me to calm down, nigga! It's not like he is a stranger, I know him! And now he is dead!"

Kalissa poked Rod with her finger, straining her voice once again. "Why did you have to kill him?"

Rod glanced back at her like she was a fly. "He knew y'all, right? Look, I'm sorry you had to see that, but I ain't going back to prison for nobody."

His eyes were so cold. She slumped back in the seat and continued to rock. Each time she closed her eyes she saw that river of black blood following her feet.

The rest of the ride was quiet. She sensed that if she had not been in the car, they would have been talking about what happened. It hit her like a ton of bricks that she didn't know these people. They had just killed someone and left him by the dumpster, just dead.

"Hey, you a'ight?" Nigel asked.

That stupid question wasn't even worth opening her eyes to. She just wanted to get home, get in her bed and hope that this had all been a dream. One thing was for sure: she never wanted to see Nigel again after this, no matter how good his sex was.

Feeling his eyes were still on her, she continued rocking and humming with her eyes closed. Her grandmother always told her if she lay down with dogs, she would get fleas. It was a tick on her tonight.

When Rod turned into her parking lot she opened the door before the car came to a halt. Kalissa jumped out, landing on the asphalt. She had forgotten about her foot. Her big toe was three times its regular size and hurt like hell. Embarrassed as hell but not wanting to show it, she grabbed the door and lifted herself up.

"C'mon, lil' baby," Nigel said before picking her up like a baby and carrying her up the stairs.

She snuggled in his neck, his cologne smelling so good she almost lost her resolve. He took her keys out of her purse, opened the door and carried her into the bedroom. He placed her on the bed and slid her zipper halfway down.

"Don't touch me." She slapped his hands away.

Nigel cocked his head to the side. "Hold up, lil' mama. I'm just trying to help your ass get out of your dress. Do it yo' damn self then."

"I will. I didn't ask for your help. Get out of my room!" She flung her pump at him, missing his head by inches.

"Yo, you crazy," Nigel mumbled, walking out of the room.

Kalissa grabbed her night clothes from under her pillow and hopped out of the room, into the bathroom. She was glad that Jamila was spending the week with Terry's parents, but if the daughter had stayed home, Kalissa would have never gone to the club.

She covered her mouth to stop herself from screaming, but her pee kept streaming in the toilet, like, forever. She looked over and realized she was out of toilet tissue. She held her head with both hands, but refused to ask for some damn tissue. Instead she grabbed her washcloth off the towel rack and wiped.

Night clothes on, teeth brushed, and face washed, not even murder could stop her nightly routine, she hopped out of the bathroom. Nigel and Rod were talking low, she heard the murmurings, but didn't even care to eavesdrop.

That blood! It stayed behind her eyelids as she forced herself to see something else. Humming "Unbreak My Heart" by Toni Braxton, she willed a picture of the ocean. Her mind filled with the waves of blue water, sand squishing between her toes and the sting of saltwater. Nodding off, she felt her bed move slightly.

"Get your ass out of here," she mumbled sleepily.

"Be quiet, I'm not going anywhere. Just go to sleep," Nigel said softly.

His hand went to her hip and she jerked away, but she was too tired and enticed by the thought of sleep to argue with him.

Once again her Grammy came to her in comfort. This time she was dressed professionally with her hair in a neat ball on top of her head. Reaching her hand out as if to soothe her pain, her mouth barely opened, but the words were loud and forever ingrained in her heart.

"Sometimes the strongest bonds are not made from love or blood, but by experiences and the secrets kept. These are the people you will always keep close to you, to protect all that is owned and who you are."

The sun glinted dangerously through the blinds as Kalissa rolled over feeling the warmth of Nigel's body. Drawn to his warmth, she cuddled next to him, until the events of the previous night came roaring back. Her eyes flew open and she pushed away from him.

"Good morning. I see you finally woke up."

She glanced over at his light brown eyes, feeling the urge to just lie in his arms and cry. Instead, she said: "I barely slept! I want you and your damn cousin out of here, now!"

As she swung her feet off the bed, an ice pack hit the floor hard. It was still cold. She shook her head, not caring if Nigel kept her foot iced up or not. She was done with his ass!

"Don't move too quick. Yo' toe isn't as swollen, but you don't know if it's fractured or not."

Chuckling, she looked back at him. "Oh, now you a doctor? You and that nigga up front just killed a man, but now yo' ass a doctor? Nigga, please!"

As soon as her foot hit the floor, an excruciating pain shot all the way up her calf. She clenched her fist and hobbled slowly to the bathroom.

***

143

Nigel walked to the front of the apartment, shaking his head. Rod was posted by the window peeping out the blinds.

"Man, she tripping. She wants us to leave." Nigel stretched, looking towards the back.

"I know she's upset, but we got to make sure she ain't calling nobody as soon as we leave. Once we get that clear, we out." Rod sucked on a toothpick.

"She say she's upset, but the way she was snoring, I can't tell. Then gonna have the nerve to say her ass couldn't sleep. She shitting me! Shiid, you and me spent more time looking out the window for blue lights while she was Sleeping Beauty." Nigel shook his head. "Then she woke up cussing me out."

"Shh!" Rod looked towards the back.

They heard drawers slamming, the sound ringing out like something hard being thrown.

"Let me talk to her," Rod said.

"Go right 'head."

Before long, they heard her walking up. When she appeared Nigel noticed a difference. Her back was straight, although she was slightly limping. Her swag was on, but he felt a sadness radiating around her. Kalissa's hair was piled up messily on her head and she had put on some green sweats and an oversized tee shirt. Rolling her eyes at both of them, she started talking before Rod could open his mouth.

"Looka here, I want y'all to hear me good. Last night never happened. I don't care how much street cred y'all need, none of us will ever speak on it again."

They both looked at her. Rod's mouth hung open.

"But—" Rod started.

She held her hand up and cut him off. "I promise, if y'all do, I will sing. I will throw your ass on top of the bus, under the bus and will roll over you twice. I don't give a fuck, 'cuz I have a daughter to raise."

She narrowed her eyes and looked directly at Rod. "And I also don't give a shit about you not wanting to go back to prison. You'll go before I will. And don't think I'm scared of you either,

144

'cuz if you try to threaten me or touch me, between my friends, my Daddy and uncles, your folks will be looking for you until hell freezes over. Capiche?"

Rod laughed so hard his shoulders shook. He steepled his hands in front of his face and nodded at her. "I was 'bout to tell you the same thing, about not running yo' damn mouth."

"Humph, you don't have to tell me nothing. Now, like I said before, y'all get your asses out my place. Matter of fact, since ya'll know the owner of the club, go make sure he doesn't have cameras. 'Cuz if he does, you looking at the new Whitney Houston."

"Girl, you crazy," Rod said as he stood, but respect shone in his eyes.

"Not crazy, but I'm gonna always protect what's mine. I guarantee you that."

C.D. Blue

CHAPTER 18

Leaving the back of the convenience store, Taj took a deep breath. After stocking his re-up, he needed to get with his crew to see what they needed, but instead he was headed to Zandra's for her 'emergency'. Business had been going well, which meant he hadn't spent much time with her. He could have, but he had been thinking about breaking it off with her.

Lissa's ongoing relationship with Nigel and even Rod's romance with his woman made Taj think it was about time he got serious with someone.

Chuckling to himself, he knew everyone thought he and Zandra were serious, but that wasn't the case; he would never wife her. She looked good enough, didn't hang out in the streets, and said she loved him.

If he was being honest, he knew that Zandra didn't start paling in comparison until Lissa got with Nigel. Ever since that night at Fefe's, that nigga hadn't left her side. Taj was low key jealous, but happy for his friend at the same time. As much as she said she loved him, Zandra's eyes didn't light up like Lissa's did when she saw Nigel and she wasn't even in love with that nigga.

Pulling in Zandra's driveway, he decided once she told him her emergency, he would break it off. He checked his pocket to see how much cash he had, because he was sure that was what she wanted.

He went to the door.

"Hey, Tee! How you doing?" Mrs. Banks exclaimed at the door.

"I'm good. How are you?"

Licking her lips while giving him the once-over, she finally answered, "I'm good, baby, real good."

"Where's Zan?"

"She's back in her room. But Tee, don't be blowing her back out, 'cuz her daddy is home and he won't like that." She laughed softly.

Shaking his head, he walked in the direction of Zandra's room. He was surprised that her dad was home, because that man worked two jobs to allow his wife enough time to fuck her boss daily. Everyone in town knew about it, there was no way Mr. Banks was as clueless as he seemed.

Zandra was sitting on her bed, watching television. Looking up in surprise, she motioned for him to close the door.

"What up, Zan? I got a lot of work to do, so spit it out," he said sitting on the edge of the bed.

"Damn! Why you always so short with me? If that damn Lissa call you with an emergency, you spend all the time she needs with her problems!" She frowned at him.

Rolling his eyes, Taj looked at her. With no make-up, no weave or wig and wearing short shorts with a flat ass, save for her tits, Zandra wasn't that pretty. Beyond everything else, it was her attitude that made her the most unattractive. Yep, it was time to let her go.

"What does Lissa have to do with anything? But anyway, Lissa doesn't have an emergency every fuckin' week. What's the problem?"

His aggravation rose as he saw the tears before they even fell. Taking big gulps, she cried and covered her face with her hands.

"I'm pregnant! Since my emergency ain't shit! I'm pregnant!"

Each word hit him like a ton of bricks. Not now . . . not with her! This was all he could think.

"Wait a minute! I thought you told me you was on the pill?" Anger started swirling around in his head.

She shrugged. "I guess a miss a few of them. You know the pill isn't one hundred percent anyway."

Watching her twist the bottom of her tee shirt nervously just made him angrier. "Well, make an appointment."

"An appointment? For what? 'Cuz I know damn well you ain't saying what I think you are?'

"Damn straight, I am. I'm not ready for no baby, you damn shole ain't and I know yo' folks don't want no baby in their house."

The tears gushed down her cheeks as she scrunched her face into an ugly mask. "How can you ask me to kill our baby, Taj? No, you said we are in this together and I thought that meant everything!"

Taj tried another tactic, because all of her crying and ranting was driving him nuts; he lowered his voice. "We're still young, Zan. We have time to have as many babies as you want. I just don't think we ready for this right now."

He rubbed her back as she calmed down, her next words shattered him.

"I can't, Tee. I already tole my momma and she's happy. We're weren't gonna tell my daddy until after I told you. What you think she gonna say if I tell her you forcing me to get rid of it?"

"I ain't forcing you to get rid of it, but how you gonna force me to be a daddy? Don't you think that's wrong?"

Sniffling, he thought he was getting through to her. Until she opened her mouth.

"Yo' ass always over there playing with Jamila. How come you can play daddy wit' her but don't want to be one to your own seed?"

"Fuck! What is your damn problem? This ain't about Lissa! Man, you got so much hate in you, you can't think straight. I'm about to go!"

She jumped up and blocked his exit. "I'm sorry, Tee, I'm just upset. I thought you would be happy. I was remembering how happy you were when Jamila was born and I thought you would feel the same way about your own. That's why I brought Lissa up."

Taj stood there with his hands in his pockets and his mouth closed. Zandra covered her face and went into another bout of tears.

"Whatever. I'll talk to you later, I'm 'bout to go. Just think about what I said, Zan. I ain't trying to hurt you or make you cry, but I just ain't ready for a baby."

Zandra wiped her nose with the back of her hand; she stopped crying suddenly and stared at him. "There's somebody else isn't there? That's why you don't want our baby. You fucking somebody else?"

"Nah, ain't nobody else. I tell you what, just think about what I said, but you make the decision. Just let me know."

***

For what seemed like the first time in his life, Taj needed some advice. It crossed his mind that she'd lied about being on the pill and had gotten pregnant on purpose. Shaking his head, it didn't matter if she did; all that counted was that he had fucked up! Calling Lissa was out of the question, especially as he thought how much she hated Zandra. He hit Cet up instead.

"What it do?"

"Where you at? I need to holla at you."

"I'm at Longhorns, come thru," Cet said.

Longhorns was pretty deserted this time of day. He spotted Cedric immediately, since he sat at the bar. Normally Taj didn't drink during the day, but after Zandra's news, he needed it. He told Cet what was going on. Cet just listened while he ate.

"Tee, it ain't that bad. You know I got two baby mommas, I just take care of my seed and let them do whateva," Cet said with his mouth full of steak.

"Mane, I don't want to be tied to Zan for no eighteen years! I was just about to break up wit' her and she come wit' this shit. Damn!"

"Look, Tee, y'all been together for a while, don't force her to get rid of yo' baby. I'm telling you that ain't no good idea. You don't know how that might affect her either. Just let her decide and you roll wit' it."

150

Nodding, Taj mulled over Cet's words and wondered how Lissa's abortion had affected her. It had never crossed his mind and she seemed to be okay, especially now.

Suddenly Cet stopped chewing, "Look at dis shit, right here."

Taj followed Cet's eyes: there stood Zo at the door with a real light-skin skinny chick. Zo glanced over at them and smiled wickedly while making a finger gun gesture with his hand pointed at Cet.

"Dis nigga!" Cet half stood, but Taj grabbed his arm.

"Just ignore him, fam'. That's what he want," Taj reasoned.

"If he keep fucking wit' me, I'ma give him what he need," Cet mumbled.

C.D. Blue

CHAPTER 19

When the door closed, all Kalissa's bravado left her body and she collapsed on the sofa. Hot tears coursed down her face; their saltiness tingled her tongue as they slipped in her mouth unbidden. Each tear had its own story, some for the life that was lost; some were from the shame of not helping, and the rest were in self-pity. Rationally, she knew she never needed to see Nigel again, but her heart said different. The last few weeks, he had become a huge part of her life.

Instinctively, she felt the door open before she heard it. Looking up, unsure of what could be next in her mess of a life, her heart flipped when it was Nigel.

"Lissa? Damn, I knew it." Nigel rushed to her side. "That's why I told Rod to bring me back. I knew you was holding that shit in," he said as he put her in his lap.

Letting her tears flow, she trembled in his arms, wetting his shirt and hiccupping with sobs.

"He's dead, like never coming back! I mean, he wasn't a bad guy. The worst thing he probably did was to hook up with me. If I hadn't been trying to keep myself safe, he would still be alive!"

Nigel rubbed her hair while kissing her tears, he tried to soothe her. "It's not yo' fault, lil' mama."

"Yes, it is. It's just like he said to me once, I'm just a pretty wrapper with nothing inside. He was right."

"That nigga said that you? Shid, lissen baby, what if he had killed you? Would that have been better?"

"No, it wouldn't. But I can't take this back and make it better," she moaned.

"That nigga knew who you was dealing with. I hate you had to see that, but in my world, you either die or sometimes you have to dead a nigga. That just the way it goes. I don't want you to ever see it again, but if you gonna be wit' me that just how it works. As for the shit that nigga said, it ain't true. You beautiful, you're a great mom and you got some good ass pussy."

She leaned back in his lap and looked at him as if he had lost his mind. "Oh yeah?"

Nigel sucked on her lips and murmured, "Fuck yeah."

"I might be able to change your world," she said softly before sucking on his neck.

"You think you can do that?" he moaned.

Kalissa bit his sexy bottom lip, and answered, "You might be surprised at all I can do."

"Show me." He spoke innocently into her ear, his breath hot against her ear. Uncontrollable shivers ran down her spine and peaked at the center of her nature.

Kalissa threw her legs around him and faced the man that had total control of her body. She leaned in and kissed him hard, releasing all of her passion in his mouth. She darted her tongue in and out at first softly, then more insistently, wiping the tip of her tongue on the roof of his mouth. His moans were low. She loved when he moaned like that. She let her hands wander to explore his chest as if it were the first time. She pulled his shirt off; hers soon followed.

He stood and she never let him go, her arms tightly around his neck, their mouths still connected in a passionate dance. Walking down the hallway, he dropped her on the bed once they entered her room. Wiggling out of her pants, she kept her eyes on the prize and moaned softly when his dick came into sight.

Kalissa knelt on the bed and playfully stuck her tongue out; Nigel came to her willingly. Licking the underside of his dick, she teased the head with licks, soft suck and barely grazed it with her teeth before taking him in her mouth. Bobbing her head to an unheard-of beat, she went down as far she could, sucking his dick harder when she made it back to the tip. His fingernails grazed her back, as she continued stroking his dick with her hand. She went lower to suck his balls, licking that tender spot underneath them. Each time she repeated this, he moaned louder.

"Fuck! you love this dick, don't you?'

Nodding, she sucked him harder while stroking his long balls before once again taking them in her mouth.

"Damn, baby, let me taste you."

She lay back, spreading her legs. He licked her slit with the tip of his long ass tongue, dragging it out until her back arched with the need to feel him inside of her.

She pressed her knees against her chest and he slid in slowly, but each stroke got harder and harder until he hammered her pussy while pushing her knees to her shoulders.

"Let me clean yo' dick off, baby."

Feeling it harden inside of her, he obliged as he watched her suck her juices off his hardness. The sight of his piercing brown eyes upon her made her cream her thighs! Kalissa turned away from him and got on her knees, ready. Nigel swiped his hardness rapidly against her slit and slammed his dick in her, slowly teasing her with the head as he playfully threatened to remove her joy. A grunt escaped his mouth each time he filled her pussy with his long dick.

As his strokes increased in intensity he pulled her ponytail holder off. Pulling her hair roughly, he asked, "Whose pussy is this?"

Kalissa arched her back, throwing her pussy back at him to match his rhythm, she choked out, "Yours, baby, it's all yours."

Nigel slapped her ass hard, "It better be. Can't nobody else touch this pussy, you understand?"

When his hand hit her ass, sending sensations through her whole body, making her quiver and shake uncontrollably, she couldn't even answer.

"Here I cum, baby, arghhh!" he moaned loudly as their bodies shook the entire bed.

***

"Girl, did you hear about what happened to Brian?" her coworker Rayven asked her as soon as she walked in the door.

"Brian? No, what happened?"

"He got killed the other night." She smacked her lips with each word.

Kalissa forced a shocked look and threw her hand over her mouth. "You lying! What happened?"

"Somebody shot him and threw his ass in a dumpster," Rayven said, shaking her head. "Girl, I didn't even know Brian was living like that, ump, humph."

Tear welled in Kalissa eyes while she kept her mouth covered; Rayven took notice and put her arm around Kalissa's shoulders.

"Girl, I'm sorry! I forgot y'all was seeing each other a lil' while ago." Rayven handed her a napkin.

Thankfully, she didn't have to force tears; they came willingly. Brian, with his hand out asking for help, popped in her head and the river flowed.

"Oh my! I didn't know. This is so terrible," she croaked as she dabbed her eyes.

Rayven rubbed her shoulders, clucking her tongue in sympathy. Her closeness and the rubbing was driving Kalissa crazy so she stepped away.

"I hate I ruined your day, I can tell you enjoyed your days off," Rayven said slyly.

"What you mean?"

"Them hickeys on your neck! That new man you got shole love sucking on you."

Kalissa had forgotten about the hickeys Nigel gave her out of lust, and to cover the bruises Brian had left on her neck.

"Girl, I'm okay, I've got to clock in before I'm late. Thank you."

"Hey, I guess you heard," Torrey hit her up as soon as she rounded the corner.

"Yes, it's just awful," she said into the napkin.

"You didn't know about it?"

Shaking her head, she still talked with the napkin covering her mouth and nose, "No, not until I got here."

"Well, I know y'all were dating. When was the last time you talked to him?"

"We were never dating, more like fooling around once or twice. We had stopped that a while ago and that's why he stopped talking to me." This nigga was really trying to pry some info out of her!

Wiping her nose one last time before throwing the napkin in the trash and checking her face in the mirror, she turned but Torrey blocked her path.

"If you need to take some time off I understand and I can cover for you."

"Nope, I'm fine. I mean, it's a terrible thing, but I can work. It's not as if I was that close to him, no more than anybody else who works here." She challenged him with her eyes.

He backed off, shrugging, letting her pass. When she made it to the front everyone seemed to be whispering and looking at her. Feeling self-conscious, but not showing it, she went about her usual tasks.

"I don't know why he would have been hanging out at that club. Somebody always getting shot up there," were some of the murmurings she heard behind her.

"I didn't even think he clubbed like that. Humph, guess you never really know people."

Her toe began throbbing and she wished that she had taken Torrey's up on leaving.

"Your rise in power will serve you losses. Do whatever it takes to protect the ones closest to your heart."

Hearing her grammy's voice again made her square her shoulders and get through her shift.

C.D. Blue

CHAPTER 20

As much as she hated the 'life' the more time she spent with Nigel, the more involved she became. Weekly get-togethers that included Rod, Nigel, Taj, Cet, Desi and Duke had become the norm. Sometimes Fefe showed up, but those were usually just fun times.

Mainly, she just listened, happy to be with Nigel. Admittedly, her respect for Rod had grown, but every now and then she added her two cents. It felt good that they appreciated her input, but most times she tried to stay away from advice, because she didn't want to know too much.

The get-togethers usually happened at her place after Jamila went to sleep. It still amazed her how well Nigel dealt with her, and Jamila had grown attached. Very attached. It was a rare occasion for her to take Jamila to the house he shared with Rod; too many niggas and she knew anything could pop off, so she didn't even go over there by her herself that often. Just enough to know that she was his woman.

Taj was having trouble with the college crew; since they went all over the state with product, other people felt as if they were cutting into profits.

"Man, we was at 'Skegee the other night and this big ass nigga tried to run us out of there," Desi complained.

"Who was it?" Taj asked.

"Homeboy introduced us to his AK, we didn't need no other introductions," Duke laughed.

"Damn, y'all just left?" Rod shook his head.

"Man, dude had five other niggas with their friends there, so hell yeah we left," Desi answered. "But we had already sold out, so somebody in that party was snitching."

"Hell yeah, 'cuz they knew we was from the Gump," Duke finished.

Taj looked worried. "I'll talk to Unc' about it soon. Until then, stay out of 'Skegee. It's small potatoes anyway, 'cuz all they want is weed and not enough for this shit."

"Y'all need to up your numbers when you go out of town, that's all. Get a few of your boys to take them trips with you. It just mean you growing, that's all," Rod spoke in that quiet way that commanded attention

"That'll leave too many areas here losing money, unless we hire some folks." Desi looked to Taj.

"Just switch up. They know y'all now. Get somebody else to go or tell the person who hooked y'all up to meet you before the parties," Lissa said, looking up.

Taj and Cedric smiled widely as if she had said something brilliant. "Yep, that makes the most sense, but I'm still gonna talk to Unc'. Lissa, you sure you don't want to be a part of my crew?" Taj teased.

"Nah, mane. I got first dibs on her joining up wit' us," Rod laughed.

"Hell nah, y'all ain't getting my baby mixed up in the game. I have other plans for her," Nigel said quickly, rubbing her shoulders.

Sitting on the floor between Nigel's legs, she looked up at him for a kiss.

"Aw shit, here we go with this!" Cedric exclaimed.

Their laughter was cut short by Fefe coming in, loud as ever.

"I heard y'all laughing all the way outside! What's good, boos?"

As usual, Fefe wore her too little clothes—spandex pants with a short sweater, but her make-up and hair was on point. A short red bob was her do for this week, which brought attention to her cheekbones.

"Lissa, when's the last time you seen Terry?' Fefe asked once she sat down.

Frowning at the sound of his name, she snapped. "I haven't, why?"

"I just asked. He is Jamila's father." She smacked her lips after each word.

Kalissa looked at her friend. "I know that, you know it, eve-rybody here know that shit, but he doesn't seem to care. So why the fuck is you coming at me like that?"

Fefe must have forgotten that Kalissa took no prisoners when it came to hoes. Period.

Fefe seemed to shrink back in her seat, she shrugged. "I just wanted to make sure he could still see her. I wasn't coming at you no type of way."

Lissa stood up, but she felt Nigel's hands slide down from her back to her butt. With a glare at Fefe, she stomped to the kitchen. After grabbing a beer out of the fridge, she stood in front of her girlfriend.

"Nah, you was being low-key petty. I don't know what's wrong wit' you, but don't come for me unless I call ya, and I ain't called yo' ass."

"Come here, baby and calm down," Nigel patted his lap.

Before she settled down comfortably, Fefe shot off at the mouth again.

"I don't know why you getting so bent out of shape, I'm sure your new lil' boyfriend know you got a baby daddy. I mean you do have a baby." Fefe made the duck lips as she finished.

Kalissa jumped out of Nigel's lap, but she felt his hand brush against her arm; however, she was too quick.

"What is wrong wit' you? Your period must be on." Kalissa said, as she stood in front of Fefe.

"Whoa, y'all stop!" Taj intervened standing between the two women.

Chest heaving, Kalissa felt Nigel and Rod behind her, Nigel with his hand on her shoulder, Rod just standing there. If Fefe said one more slick thing, she was ready to slap the taste out of her mouth.

"You know, I didn't mean all that, I'm sorry Lissa. I don't know what's wrong wit' me. I'll leave if you want me too." Fefe looked contrite, but her body language was still stiff.

"Calm down, lil' mama, let's jus' have a good time," Nigel said in her ear, licking her earlobe.

"I don't care if you stay or go, but say some more petty ass shit, I'ma beat yo' ass like I used to when we were kids. I don't care how big yo' ass done got."

"Ooooo, damn!" That came from Desi, laughing in the corner.

Tears glistened in Fefe's eyes; Kalissa noticed them but didn't care. She shouldn't have started that shit.

"Why women have to be at each other all the time? I don't understand that shit! Y'all been friends forever and let some petty shit have y'all at blows, shit!" Taj looked between the two women.

"Right, long enough for her to know that I would never keep my baby away from her daddy on purpose, humph. Matter of fact, let me go check and make sure you didn't wake her up wit' yo' foolishness." Kalissa walked out of the room and went to the back.

"What the fuck is wrong wit' you, Fe?" Taj said under his breath angrily.

"What? I jus' asked a question, I didn't mean no harm," Fefe said defensively.

"Naw, you was dead wrong for that shit, Fe. And you know it," Nigel said.

Hearing it from him seemed to shame her. She dropped her head to study her fingernails. Taj noticed the strange way Rod looked at her, but dismissed it because he didn't know the women's history like Taj did.

Kalissa walked back up outwardly calmer, but she ignored Fefe as she went back to her place on Nigel's lap. The skepticism Taj had felt when Kalissa and Nigel got together was gone. He actually liked them together now, Nigel seemed to have a calming effect on her and he took care of her. Even Cet seemed okay with it.

"I got some cards." Desi held up a deck of cards, smiling.

"Boy, if you don't put them cards down, ain't nobody losing wit' you tonight." Kalissa laughed.

Desi won her over and they drank, played cards. Nigel and Rod left to go get more beer, so that most of them were toasted. Except Kalissa, who hadn't drunk much of anything.

"Hey we 'bout to head out," Cedric made an announcement after his last loss.

"Wait. I want to play one mo' hand," Desi, who had been on a winning streak, said.

"Aren't you too drunk to drive, Cet? Y'all can sleep on the floor here, as long as you gone before Jamila gets up," Kalissa offered.

Knowing Cedric, it was obvious he was drunk. He wasn't staggering but professed he loved everyone. He always declared he loved everyone, when he was drunk.

'I'm good and ain't no way I'm sleeping on the floor when I got a bed waiting on me. But I love you for that," he blubbered.

Cedric walked over to Kalissa with his arms out, but Nigel stopped him.

"Alright now, love her from where you at, nephew," Nigel laughed. "Don't be hugging on my woman."

"Aw, mane! You know it ain't like that, but I gotcha."

"Y'all sure you don't want to stay? Cet, you are drunk, 'cuz you about to tell my man you loved him," Kalissa smiled.

"We outta here! Come on," Cet laughed.

Saying their goodbyes, they left.

***

"Man, I would have slept on her floor," Desi complained.

"Me too," Duke agreed from the back seat.

"Mane, y'all ain't even driving. Her nigga wasn't going for that. I'm not sleeping on no floor, when I got a bed and some wet wet waiting on me," Cet said.

Quieting down, Cet started thinking about the woman he met a few days ago, her pussy was fire and he was going to just show up! Thinking about it made him speed up some as he rode down Fairview Avenue. Once they were past the shops and got to the darkened roads leading to the boulevard, he wished he had gone the quicker way. This route had less cops, which meant less chances of a DUI.

"Mane, slow down, you gonna make me throw up!" Duke sputtered.

"Nigga, throw up in my ride if you dare! What the hell?"

Cet noticed a car or truck right up on him with their bright lights on. He sped up some more and the car stayed with him. Then suddenly, it veered to the left and as soon as it got beside him he knew he had fucked up. He slammed on brakes a little too late.

Plat! Plattt! Plattt! Plattt! Plattt! Platt!

Turning the wheel wildly, he felt the hot pain of a graze on his arm and he knew that the brakes had saved his life. Cet ran up on the side of the road and heard Duke screaming.

"Desi! Desi! Say something, man!"

Once his vehicle stopped, he looked over and saw Desi with blood burbling out of his mouth, making a gurgling sound. Pressing the gas, he maneuvered out of the grass, keeping his eye out for the other vehicle as he sped to the hospital.

***

"Aye, mane, if your guys need a lil' mo' fire power when they go out of town, just hit me up. We fam' now, we all need to eat," Rod said as Taj prepared to leave.

"That's what up! Fasho, I'll do that," Taj smiled before rolling his eyes as his phone rang.

"What up?" His eyes grew large. "What? Where y'all at? Aww man, nooo! I'll be right there."

"What happened?" Kalissa asked as she, Fefe, Nigel and Rod stood in suspense.

Tears gathered in Taj's eyes, "Desi got shot, it's bad. I gotta go."

"What!" they all cried in unison.

Taj held his head and headed to the door. Kalissa stood with her hand over her mouth. Seeing Taj so upset, she knew he didn't need to go alone.

164

"Wait, I'll drive you! You don't need to drive like that," Kalissa hollered.

"She's right, Taj. I'll stay here with Jamila, Lissa," Fefe said with tears running down her face.

Kalissa gave her a quick tight hug, all earlier disagreements forgotten. "Thanks, girl."

"We'll follow y'all," Rod said.

Riding to the hospital was a somber affair. Tears pricked the back of Kalissa's eyes as she prayed that Desi made it.

"Lord, he's just a kid, please have mercy if it's your will." she said silently.

Glancing over at Taj, he just kept slamming his hand on the dashboard.

"This is so fucked up! I should have made them stay! They had just said ole dude pulled up on them. Damn!" was all he kept saying over and over.

"Tee, it ain't your fault. None of us knew this would happen, we couldn't have known," Kalissa croaked out over the big lump in her throat.

Taj just shook his head.

Once they made it to the hospital, running in, they noticed all the black and whites around the Emergency Room entrance. After moving through the metal detector, they looked around the waiting room. It was crowded, but no sign of Cedric or Duke. Taj ran to the window and as he asked the lady about his friends, Lissa hung behind him. The door from the back opened and Duke came through.

His tee shirt was soaked with blood, and it had spattered on his arms and pants. Noticing Kalissa first, he walked to her dazed and hugged her tight, his body shaking with sobs.

"My brother is gone, they killed my brother! He's gone, Lissa, he's gone!"

Holding him tightly, he shook in her arms, his brother's blood binding them together as she tried to absorb his pain. The tears that had been stuck in her throat rushed out, and she could only cry with him; there were no words to say. Taj walked over and wrapped his arms around both of them, and that's how they stayed for a long time.

CHAPTER 21

Desi's death hit them all hard. It was as if a light had gone out. Cedric was out for blood, Duke was heartbroken, and Taj was different.

A few days before the funeral, he and Kalissa sat on her steps, watching Jamila play outside and talking. Later she would realize it was the last conversation she had with the Taj she knew.

"Lissa, it wasn't supposed to be like this. You know this is one of the reasons I never wanted to fool with the crack game," Taj said with a huge sigh. "I just wanted my niggas to make some money, get ahead and live! Not worrying about territories and getting shot."

She let him ramble on, because she felt as if he needed to get it off his chest. She just listened and nodded. She reached down to pat his shoulder and passed him the blunt.

"Desi was so smart, he wasn't even planning on staying in the game long. Damn! He told me he just wanted to make enough to get his momma straight, then he was going back to school."

"Wow! I didn't know that. It's just so sad, I keep seeing his smile. Damn! Tee, maybe you just take this as a sign to get out. I don't even want to think about something like this happening to you," Kalissa's voice cracked.

Taj glanced back up at her, he smiled sadly. "Whether you know it or not, a lot people depend on me now for their money. I'll be a'ight."

"Your uncle can put them with somebody else or get some-body else to take your spot. It's just been so much death lately," she ended, sad.

"Shidd, I know. That's right I heard about yo' ole boy. Damn, that was messed up. Did they ever say what that was about?" Passing the blunt back to her, he kept looking at her.

"Not that I've heard." The smoke was in her face and she glad for a reason to squint. As close as she was to Taj, there were some things to never speak on.

"Damn! That's two funerals almost back to back. We too young for this shit! I remember being little thinking that only old people died. Shid, I was stupid!"

"It wasn't *stupid*. It's just the environment we grew up in," she murmured.

There was no need to correct anything about Brian's funeral; she didn't go. Once they announced it, she thought about it, but nixed that idea. With the knowledge of exactly how his last moments went—and knowing that they were burying him because he had the misfortune to have feelings for her—was too much. People at work were still whispering about her, calling her the ice queen, a cold ass bitch, along with other names she hadn't heard about it. As long as they didn't say it to her face, she just ignored them.

"How's Cedric?" she asked, changing the subject. Taj had known her too long and any crack in her poker face, he would notice.

"Ready to kill someone. You know the bullet that grazed him got Desi, along with another one. I ain't never seen him like this."

"He'll probably never be the same, and Duke as well. Death changes so much because it's final. You can't come back from that." She moved her shoulders to the beat as a Mercedes pulled up playing "ASAP" by TI, loudly.

Shocked to see Nigel step out of the vehicle, she smiled when he picked up a squealing Jamila. Her baby was crazy about Nigel, just like her momma.

"What up?" he spoke to Taj, before looking at Kalissa with a grin.

"Whose car is that?" Kalissa asked while standing up.

"Rod just bought it. I'm putting it on the road right for him," Nigel said with a big wink.

"I'ma head out. I need to catch up with Cet and see what he got going on." Taj stood, dusting off.

Kalissa walked down the one step that separated them, and hugged him lightly. "Be safe."

"I will." He put his hand over his heart as he walked down the stairs.

Taj walked away with a slight slump in shoulders. Kalissa noticed it and tears formed in her eyes again. Since Desi died it seemed as if she cried daily.

Sitting on Nigel's shoulders, Jamila asked, "Mommy why you crying?"

"I'm not crying, I have something in my eyes," Kalissa smiled slightly as she swiped her face.

"I bet if we take yo' mommy to the mall that might make her happier," Nigel said in a loud whisper to Jamila.

"I don't know how you knew," she grinned through her tears.

Shopping didn't make her feel as good as she thought it would, especially since they were mainly buying funeral clothes. It wasn't as if she could show up in one of her club dresses. She picked out a simple fitted black dress by Prada; it still cost more than all of her clothes put together.

It was a lie that men didn't take long shopping! Nigel kept picking up slacks, putting them back down, then going back to them, she was tired from nodding. Finally, he decided on the first pair of black slacks, with a black shirt and tie. Jamila was too happy to get three outfits and some toys, which was good since Kalissa's dad was picking her up the next day.

Her Grammy enjoyed the little princess's company so much she wanted to get her all the time and got mad when Kalissa told her no.

After going out to eat, they finally made it back to her place. As Kalissa watched Nigel with her baby, she realized she loved him. Completely. Once Jamila went to sleep they made love all night long.

***

The funeral was packed, but a somber affair. There were people from all walks of life. Young people, dressed down, church people, professionals, teachers, the entire dope crew from

Montgomery, including Taj's uncle, hoodrats, and even some fiends.

His service was held at Beulah Baptist Church, which was a large church, but there still weren't enough seats. The outpouring of love was overwhelming.

They did the morbid walk around to see him lying in the casket. He looked like a kid. Kalissa's breath caught in her throat as she thought of the many times they laughed, teased and talked. Nigel nudged her to move on because she was holding up the line. Touching his hand, she walked off but stopped to hug Duke and Cet.

Once they sat down, Kalissa was squished between Nigel and Rod's girlfriend. Taj, Zandra and his uncle sat in the pew in front of them. Fefe was behind them, because she had been late getting there. They were all hung-over from the night before. Hanging out talking about the times they remembered with Desi, until late the night before.

Tears from death shook most people and there was plenty, but Kalissa held strong until a woman got up and sang, "The Battle Is The Lord's". That did it for Kalissa. She grabbed a tissue from Rod's girlfriend and wiped her face as her tears fell with no fanfare.

"You a'ight, baby?" Nigel whispered as he wiped the corners of his eyes.

Nodding, she pulled herself together, only to lose it again, when they closed the casket and Desi's mom tried to get to it, screaming and crying.

"*Nooooo!!* Not my baby, I can't leave him alone in there! *Nooooo!* Why they took my baby from me?"

Cedric, Duke and another male family member pulled her back to her seat. Her haunted cries could be heard throughout the rest of the service. Kalissa looked down and just let her tears fall. It was so heartbreaking she just wanted to leave.

"I got you, lil' mama." Nigel pulled her close and kissed the side of her forehead.

Finally, it was over! Nigel hung back, talking to some people. Kalissa needed some air. She walked outside, noticing some of the crowd had dispersed, but many stood around talking, while others hugged and comforted the family. Almost tripping on the cobblestone, she caught herself, looking back to see if anybody had seen her.

An eerie sense of déjá vu hit her. Everything she looked at, she'd seen before. She closed her eyes to rid herself of the sensation; when she opened them, it was back to normal.

She saw Taj and Cedric standing beside Taj's car, talking intently. Cedric was motioning with his hands while Taj kept holding his hand up as if to stop what Cet was saying. Wondering what they were talking about, she noticed Duke standing off by himself at the end of the family car. Hoping that awful sensation didn't return, she walked gingerly over to him. He met her halfway and crushed her in an embrace.

Pulling away, she looked at him. His eyes were fire-red, swollen from the many tears she knew he had shed.

"I wish we had listened to you that night and stayed at your place." He laughed without humor. "That's what we were talking about right before it happened. How we should have listened to you . . ." His voice trailed off at the end.

From out of nowhere, words that hadn't crossed her mind came out of her mouth. "Well, listen to me now. Get out. This is not the life for you, Duke. Go back to school, get a job, do something, just get out. Don't put your momma through this again."

With his mouth hanging open, Duke looked at her strangely, then he hugged her again, whispering in her ear, "I'm listening to you this time, I promise. I am."

As they stepped away from one another, tears blurred her vision. "Just keep in touch."

"You don't have to worry about that. You'll always be right here!" He slapped the palm of his hand against the left side of his chest.

Kalissa turned and walked to Taj's car, she curled her lip upward when she spotted Zandra getting out of the passenger side. Seeing Cedric looking so broken changed her attitude.

"Hey," she said softly, hugging him gently as to not hurt his arm.

"Hey, thank y'all for coming, it means a lot." Cet looked towards the cars moving out. "I guess I need to catch up with the family to go to the cemetery."

Watching him walk off, Taj, Zandra and Lissa stood awkwardly together. Spotting Nigel, Kalissa took that as her cue to leave, so she hugged Taj and even gave Zandra a side hug.

"That was a tough one," Nigel said as they got into his black BMW.

"Yes, it was," she murmured looking at him.

He looked like a million dollars to her and the all black just highlighted his latte complexion. Sad as the occasion was, she was still proud to be on his arm, so the small smile that lit her face was natural.

"I got you a tee shirt," he said suddenly.

"A tee shirt? What kind of tee shirt?"

"With Desi on it. A guy was selling them," he said, never looking at her because he was too busy weaving in and out of traffic.

"At the funeral? That's tacky. Thank you. I'll keep it but I won't wear it." She smacked her lips.

"Why not?"

"Nah, I just don't believe in that," she said quietly and left it at that.

"Lil' mama, you crazy," he laughed.

There weren't many people at the cemetery, but enough that had a good hike to get to the site. Once that was over, people really stood around chopping it up with each other. Lissa, Nigel and Rod stood off to the side, when the same good-looking guy from the club walked up.

"What up, mane? I ain't seen you in a minute!" he said to Rod.

172

They dapped it up then he looked over and covered his mouth with his fist, laughing.

"Ayye! Nigel, nigga where yo' ass been hiding?" The dude gave Nigel a man hug and noticed Kalissa.

"I be's around, yo' ass the one be missing from the spot."

"This you, mane?"

"Yeah, Rollo, this is Kalissa," Nigel introduced them.

Rollo! The guy from the red light! That's why he looked familiar! There was no doubt that he was fine, he had his dreads in two braids and wore a black shirt under a grey vest and that huge chain around his neck. He took her hand and shook it lightly.

"A queen." His eyes twinkled, so she knew he remembered her too.

"Nice to meet ya," she said simply with a smile.

"Hold up, mane, you holding her hand too long." Nigel laughed moving in front her, breaking the connection.

While they talked, Kalissa began people-watching. Family members were huddled together. She saw an old man trying to chat up a younger woman, at the cemetery, for crying out loud! Taj was closer to the family with Zandra stuck up his butt; Lissa caught herself rolling her eyes.

The one person she didn't see was Fefe and it would be hard to miss her. Scanning the rest of the crowd her, eyes fell on a familiar face standing off by himself. Zo!

The nigga was probably standing on somebody's grave, with his stupid ass. Just standing there, not interacting with anybody, looking out of place. The stupid look on his face reminded her of when they were younger. Zo had stolen some money out of one of their classmates' purse. No one could prove it, but Kalissa knew it was him from the way he acted and seemed. Just like he was standing there looking!

Narrowing her eyes at him, it hit her that he was behind Desi's murder. His threat to Cedric that night at her apartment rang in her ears. Trying to shake those thoughts away, she tuned back into the conversation going on beside her.

"I didn't know him, but," Rollo glanced Kalissa's way, "when ole dude tole me about it, I came to give my respect. He was fam', ya know? Some of my crew knew him, but the main one didn' wanna come!"

"Damn, that's fucked up," Rod said.

"Yeah, mane, he jus' wit' me 'cuz he ole dude fam', real fam'. He a'ight, but otha than that I wouldn't fuck wit' him, for real," Rollo said.

Kalissa looked back at Zo; he was staring at her, with a smirk.

"Smile now, nigga 'cuz one day I'ma fuck you up." Kalissa muttered the promise quietly.

CHAPTER 22

They all congregated at Taj's place that night. It was a different scene from their other get-togethers. Everybody was quiet and it felt strange without Desi and Duke. Music played softly in the background, but nobody was paying it any attention.

Zandra and Fefe acted like long lost cousins when they saw one another; Kalissa just shook her head. It didn't matter that Fefe was still friends with the bitch, but they didn't have to act that damn happy to see each other.

Kalissa had promised Taj that she would be nice to Zandra. That just meant not saying anything to her, but she noticed how Zandra kept looking at her. Kalissa just rolled her eyes and ignored her.

Cedric walked around drinking out of a bottle of Crown Royal, zoning out. Not knowing what to say to him, Lissa just kept quiet, hoping that one day he would forgive himself.

She walked to the bathroom and leaned against the door after closing it. The sadness and pallor of death was so strong she was exhausted from it. As many times as Taj had been there for her, it was her time to be his source of strength. It had to come from her, because that trifling hoe he was with wouldn't do it. Squaring her shoulders, she bounced out of the bathroom.

Nigel met her in the hallway.

"Aye pretty mama, you got a man?" Nigel's breath was wet, hot and sexy in her ear.

"Nah, but I shole would like to be yo' woman." She kissed him hard and deep.

"A'ight now, don't make me take you down to the car," he said lustfully as they walked to the front.

"Do it!" she laughed and looked right into Zandra's scowl.

Before she could open her mouth, Cet stumbled out of the kitchen, still holding on to the bottle.

"A'ight, y'all I'ma head out, need 'o check on my folks. I'll see y'all later."

"No, sir! You are not driving like that. I'll take you home," Fefe announced loudly.

"I can ma' it," Cet slurred.

"Aht! Aht! You riding wit' me and I ain't gonna say it again," Fefe said, grabbing the bottle from him and setting it on the table.

"Damn! A'ight then! You sure you wanna ride wit' me," Cedric was drunk, but still blaming himself.

"Nigga, shut up and come on!"

Cedric stumbled around, hugging everybody twice and telling them he loved them three and four times. Fefe finally got him out after he'd promised to text them once she dropped him off.

Taj, Nigel and Rod sat at the dining room table. Taj was looking thoughtful as he took the tobacco out of a Swisher.

"What's wrong, Tee?" Kalissa sat down across from him.

"I'm cool, just gotta come up wit' a plan," he said as he rolled a blunt.

"What kind of plan?" she asked, pushing the ashtray closer to him.

"I can't let this slide, Lissa. Niggas be thinking I'm weak and then my whole crew will be in jeopardy. I can't do that." With his lips turned downward, he shook his head slowly.

Taj passed the blunt to Nigel, while Rod looked real serious and mean, spoke, "You right, fam. Dese niggas are treacherous nowdays. If you don't blaze back it'll be yo' own set that will turn on you."

Kalissa looked at Taj, who seemed to be changing right before her eyes. In all her years of knowing him, she'd never known him to be violent.

Taj gave Rod a strange look. "Yo, ya right! I hadn't even thought 'bout that."

Thinking about his set, he knew a few of them that would definitely see his weakness as a rise in power.

"Y'all know who did dis?" Rod had leaned forward.

Nigel was looking at Kalissa who was knee-deep in the conversation. "Aye, let's take this outside, mane. These women don't need to hear all dis!"

"Damn, my bad, you right," Rod nodded.

"What women? I'm wit y'all," Kalissa said heatedly.

"Nah, nah, lil' mama, not wit' this, you ain't," Nigel shot her down.

Looking back towards the living room, Zandra was staring at her phone. She didn't want to be left out. Pouting, she looked at Nigel, who gave her a hard stare.

"Go on over there wit' yo' girl, we won't be long," he said to Lissa, tilting his head toward Zandra.

"Humph, she ain't my girl," Kalissa muttered.

"Go on, now," Nigel growled, giving her a little push.

Rolling her eyes, she got up and stomped over to oversized chair, away from Zan, and sat down. After hitting the blunt a few more times the men walked outside.

Once they left, the women sat in silence. Zandra was smiling in her phone, so Kalissa put her head back and closed her eyes. Zandra's boyfriend, Taj, was becoming a whole other person and this simple bitch didn't even know it.

"You know you don't have to act like you do," Zandra said with a slight laugh.

"Look, I told Tee I wouldn't start anything wit' you, that does not mean I want to talk to you," Kalissa said, never opening her eyes.

"Girl, you always tripping," Zandra said, getting up.

Kalissa looked at her through her eyelashes. Everyone else had changed clothes, but Zandra was still dressed in her church clothes. Looking more like she should have been an usher, instead of in the congregation. Wearing a black skirt suit with a white ruffled shirt and six inch heels, she looked older than all of them. She always had, though.

Once she returned from the kitchen, Zandra sat back down and blew out a heavy breath. "Taj need to come on. I'm hungry and sick of looking at you!"

Kalissa didn't open her mouth or eyes, only because of her promise. Zandra's next comment snapped her out of her tranquil state of mind.

"You act like you so perfect and ain't never made no mistakes."

Sitting straight up, Kalissa looked at her to see if she was serious. She was.

"Mistake? That's what you call fucking my boyfriend while I was pregnant?"

"Lissa, it was one time! I made a huge mistake and I said I was sorry!" Zandra sat on the edge of the sofa with her hands out.

It took three deep breaths to calm her nerves, Kalissa dismissed her with a wave of her hand and laid her head back on the chair again.

But Zandra's mouth spiraled out of control again. "You forgave his ass! And laid back down with him. Humph, but I forgot that's how you are anyway. Always running behind dick."

Kalissa was seething, she rolled her neck to pop it before she answered. "Nah, hoe, dick runs behind me. Terry told me how you chased him down. I forgave him because we had a child and furthermore you were supposed to be my friend. My best friend! You ain't shit!"

"You just been mad at me so long that you don't want to admit how much alike we are."

"Believe me, sis, we are not the same."

"You doing the same thing you hate me for," Zandra shot back.

"What? Zan, what kinda of crazy shit you talking about now?"

"You know your new boo thang been blowing Fefe's back out for years. You don't care about that! I guess it's different when you do it to a friend," Zandra smacked her lips and sat back.

Feeling all types of heat overcome her, she looked into Zandra's smug face. All types of thoughts ran through her mind. Shaking her head, she told herself that Zandra was just trying to get back at her.

"Nah, you lying! Fefe would have said something," Kalissa said, still shaking her head.

"Not when the fucking has always been a secret. Hmm, I bet you met him at Fefe's, what you think he was doing over there?" Zandra chuckled.

Kalissa bit her bottom lip as she thought about how different Fefe had been acting since she and Nigel had been together. They didn't talk as much and when Kalissa called her, she always seemed to rush off the phone. That didn't mean anything, though; she was probably busy, Kalissa rationalized. Then it crossed her mind how bitchy Fefe had acted the night Desi had gotten killed. No, it couldn't be true.

"So, while you trying to stay mad at me? You ought to understand how it happens. I bet Fefe has forgiven you."

Each word that came of Zandra's mouth was delivered with a perverse joy. Ever since she saw Kalissa with Nigel at the funeral, she'd been waiting for this moment.

"Zan, I don't believe nothing that comes out of your mouth. Anyway, Fefe told me that they were related some type of way. I already know what type of friend you are, so I guess now it's time for Fefe to find out," Kalissa said, rubbing her hands together.

Looking at her phone, Zandra sighed. "Kissing cousins I guess. That was just their cover-up. Come on, my man is ready to take me out to eat."

Zandra stood up and walked to the door. Kalissa got up slowly, following her.

"You think I'm lying? Ask yo' man about it or better yet, ask Felicia. You can tell when she's lying." She shrugged. "Or she might tell the truth. Who knows maybe y'all can be sister wives."

***

"I'll keep my ear to the streets. I know some niggas up there in Macon too, I'll ask around," Rod said to Taj as they leaned against Nigel's BMW.

"I don't know if it was them niggas out of 'Skegee, that just don't feel right," Taj said slowly.

"It don't matter, blast them anyway, that way yo' set will see you ain't playing. Do it on the strength that they drew on yo' boys."

Taj nodded, soaking in the knowledge. "Bet, that makes sense," Taj said.

Rod replied. "No worries, we got yo' back. Wit' both of our sets together, them niggas won't know what hit 'em. But right now, I'ma go spend some time wit' my woman. I'm tired of looking at y'all hard legs. I'll hit you up tomorrow." Rod laughed, turning to take his leave right away.

After Rod left, Taj and Nigel smoked in silence, both men lost in their thoughts. Nigel spoke up first.

"If you find out it's not them, blast whoever too. Then niggas will know you 'bout that life."

"Sho, you right. Let me text Zan to bring her ass down, she been waiting to eat forever! She too good for that funeral food." Taj laughed, as he sent the text.

"Lil' mama know she nosey as hell! She gonna ask me what we said as soon as we get in the car," Nigel laughed passing the blunt to Taj.

"You right, betta you than me," Taj laughed, feeling more relaxed knowing that they had a plan and from the weed.

Blop! Blop! Blop! Blop! Blop! Blop! Blop! Blop!

The sound was so loud both men jumped, looking around.

"What the hel . . ." Nigel started when they both saw Zandra hit the pavement coming off the last step. They ran in that direction. She lay still on the concrete and then they heard Kalissa running down with her hand over her mouth.

"Oh shit, Zan!" she screamed.

Nigel felt Zandra's neck for a pulse. While Taj began picking her up, Nigel stopped him.

"Nah, man, let's call the ambulance, you don't wanna move her. That might make it worse."

Taj nodded, trying to hold back the tears.

Nigel called 911.

***

Racing behind the ambulance, all Taj could think of was the condition of the baby. He was worrying about the babe now, a baby he said he didn't want. Wiping one lone tear that rolled down his face, he couldn't help but wonder if he was being punished. Slamming his hand on the steering wheel, he thought about how he told her to be careful whenever she was walking on his stairway in her high heels!

Saying a small prayer, something he hadn't done in ages, he prayed for Zandra and their baby to be alright. All the bad thoughts he had about her flew out the window as he sped to the hospital, with Nigel and Kalissa behind him. The ambulance had made it there in record time, thanks to living in a mostly white neighborhood. If he lived in the hood, they would still be waiting.

Whipping into the parking lot of the hospital, the memory of Desi's death shook him. How many more times would he have to make this kind of trip? Even though this wasn't a result of his lifestyle, but what if it was?

With a deep breath, Taj looked down at his hands sorrowfully before stepping out of the car.

It was the same type of circus at the hospital that he had encountered last time. Different woman, same bad attitude, sitting at the reception desk. After being told he would have to wait, he looked around for a seat.

Kalissa and Nigel rushed in, surrounding him and of course, Kalissa asked question after question. Finally, Nigel got her to hush and they sat there until he felt Kalissa touch his wrist lightly. He noticed her nod forwards. He followed the direction of her nod and saw Zandra's dad walking from the back.

"Damn, how did they get here so before us?" Taj wondered out loud.

"You know they live close, go talk to him, Taj. He's looking for you," Kalissa said calmly.

Zandra's dad did not look happy to see him as he approached.

"She's asking for you, but I want to know what the hell you did to my baby?" Mr. Banks whispered furiously.

"I didn't do nothing! I told her to stop wearing them heels on my stairs," Taj huffed angrily, pulling the door open to go to the back.

The smell hit him before the hustle and bustle of the back. He heard monitors beeping, people were talking fast, nurses running around and white curtains pulled closed. Mr. Banks led him halfway to the back of the room, he pushed the curtain back and his heart fell.

Zandra's face was swollen, her right eye was closed and she had a white bandage on her nose. The only part of her body he could see was her arm and leg in slings. Her mom sat beside her.

Mrs. Banks gave him a small smile, then stood. "I'll leave you two alone for a few minutes."

"For what? If she wasn't messing with this thug, she wouldn't be here," Mr. Banks roared.

"Baby, come on. Give them a few minutes, just two or three, okay?" She led him out.

Sitting beside the bed, her face was so messed up Taj couldn't tell if her eyes were opened or closed.

"Tee?" he heard her whisper.

There was nothing for him to hold and he was scared if he touched her it would hurt her.

"I'm here, Zan," he told her softly.

Tears ran down her face, she said something but it was so low he couldn't hear her.

"What'd you say?"

"Sorry," came the garbled reply.

That hit him like a ton of bricks! There was the answer about his baby. Damn!

"It's alright, we'll have another one, I promise," Seeing her like that made him forget that not only had he been about to break up with her, but also that he said he didn't want to be tied to her for long.

It looked like she tried to smile, so he threw in his own joke.

"But next time you won't be wearing no heels," he chuckled.

Once again she said something he couldn't hear.

182

For the Love of a Boss

"What was that?"
His whole world shattered at her words.
"Lissa did this. She pushed me."

To Be Continued...
For the Love of a Boss 2
Coming Soon

Submission Guideline

Submit the first three chapters of your completed manuscript to ldpsubmissions@gmail.com, subject line: Your book's title. The manuscript must be in a .doc file and sent as an attachment. Document should be in Times New Roman, double spaced and in size 12 font. Also, provide your synopsis and full contact information. If sending multiple submissions, they must each be in a separate email.

Have a story but no way to send it electronically? You can still submit to LDP/Ca$h Presents. Send in the first three chapters, written or typed, of your completed manuscript to:

LDP: Submissions Dept
Po Box 944
Stockbridge, Ga 30281

DO NOT send original manuscript. Must be a duplicate.

Provide your synopsis and a cover letter containing your full contact information.

Thanks for considering LDP and Ca$h Presents.

For the Love of a Boss

Coming Soon from Lock Down Publications/Ca$h Presents

BOW DOWN TO MY GANGSTA

By **Ca$h**

TORN BETWEEN TWO

By **Coffee**

THE STREETS STAINED MY SOUL **II**

By **Marcellus Allen**

BLOOD OF A BOSS **VI**

SHADOWS OF THE GAME II

TRAP BASTARD II

By **Askari**

LOYAL TO THE GAME **IV**

By **T.J. & Jelissa**

IF LOVING YOU IS WRONG... **III**

By **Jelissa**

TRUE SAVAGE **VIII**

MIDNIGHT CARTEL IV

DOPE BOY MAGIC IV

CITY OF KINGZ III

By **Chris Green**

BLAST FOR ME **III**

A SAVAGE DOPEBOY III

CUTTHROAT MAFIA III

DUFFLE BAG CARTEL VI

HEARTLESS GOON VI

By **Ghost**

A HUSTLER'S DECEIT III

KILL ZONE **II**

BAE BELONGS TO ME III

C.D. Blue

A DOPE BOY'S QUEEN III

By **Aryanna**

COKE KINGS V

KING OF THE TRAP II

By **T.J. Edwards**

GORILLAZ IN THE BAY V

3X KRAZY III

De'Kari

THE STREETS ARE CALLING II

Duquie Wilson

KINGPIN KILLAZ IV

STREET KINGS III

PAID IN BLOOD III

CARTEL KILLAZ IV

DOPE GODS III

Hood Rich

SINS OF A HUSTLA II

ASAD

KINGZ OF THE GAME VI

Playa Ray

SLAUGHTER GANG IV

RUTHLESS HEART IV

By **Willie Slaughter**

THE HEART OF A SAVAGE III

By **Jibril Williams**

FUK SHYT II

By **Blakk Diamond**

TRAP QUEEN

By **Troublesome**

YAYO V

For the Love of a Boss

GHOST MOB II

Stilloan Robinson

KINGPIN DREAMS III

By Paper Boi Rari

CREAM II

By Yolanda Moore

SON OF A DOPE FIEND III

By Renta

FOREVER GANGSTA II

GLOCKS ON SATIN SHEETS III

By Adrian Dulan

LOYALTY AIN'T PROMISED III

By Keith Williams

THE PRICE YOU PAY FOR LOVE III

By Destiny Skai

I'M NOTHING WITHOUT HIS LOVE II

SINS OF A THUG II

By Monet Dragun

LIFE OF A SAVAGE IV

MURDA SEASON IV

GANGLAND CARTEL IV

CHI'RAQ GANGSTAS III

By **Romell Tukes**

QUIET MONEY IV

EXTENDED CLIP III

By **Trai'Quan**

THE STREETS MADE ME III

By **Larry D. Wright**

IF YOU CROSS ME ONCE II

ANGEL III

C.D. Blue

By **Anthony Fields**
FRIEND OR FOE III
By **Mimi**
SAVAGE STORMS III
By **Meesha**
BLOOD ON THE MONEY III
By **J-Blunt**
THE STREETS WILL NEVER CLOSE II
By **K'ajji**
NIGHTMARES OF A HUSTLA III
By **King Dream**
THE WIFEY I USED TO BE II
By **Nicole Goosby**
IN THE ARM OF HIS BOSS
By **Jamila**
MONEY, MURDER & MEMORIES III
Malik D. Rice
CONCRETE KILLAZ II
By **Kingpen**
HARD AND RUTHLESS II
By **Von Wiley Hall**
LEVELS TO THIS SHYT II
By **Ah'Million**
MOB TIES II
By **SayNoMore**
BODYMORE MURDERLAND II
By **Delmont Player**
THE LAST OF THE OGS II
Tranay Adams
FOR THE LOVE OF A BOSS II

For the Love of a Boss

By C. D. Blue

Available Now

RESTRAINING ORDER **I & II**
By **CA$H & Coffee**
LOVE KNOWS NO BOUNDARIES **I II & III**
By **Coffee**
RAISED AS A GOON I, II, III & IV
BRED BY THE SLUMS I, II, III
BLAST FOR ME I & II
ROTTEN TO THE CORE I II III
A BRONX TALE I, II, III
DUFFLE BAG CARTEL I II III IV V
HEARTLESS GOON I II III IV V
A SAVAGE DOPEBOY I II
DRUG LORDS I II III
CUTTHROAT MAFIA I II
By **Ghost**
LAY IT DOWN **I & II**
LAST OF A DYING BREED I II
BLOOD STAINS OF A SHOTTA I & II III
By **Jamaica**
LOYAL TO THE GAME I II III
LIFE OF SIN I, II III
By **TJ & Jelissa**
BLOODY COMMAS I & II
SKI MASK CARTEL I II & III

189

C.D. Blue

190

For the Love of a Boss

THE STREETS BLEED MURDER **I, II & III**

THE HEART OF A GANGSTA I II& III

By **Jerry Jackson**

CUM FOR ME I II III IV V VI

An **LDP Erotica Collaboration**

BRIDE OF A HUSTLA **I II & II**

THE FETTI GIRLS **I, II& III**

CORRUPTED BY A GANGSTA I, II III, IV

BLINDED BY HIS LOVE

THE PRICE YOU PAY FOR LOVE I II

DOPE GIRL MAGIC I II III

By **Destiny Skai**

WHEN A GOOD GIRL GOES BAD

By **Adrienne**

THE COST OF LOYALTY I II III

By Kweli

A GANGSTER'S REVENGE **I II III & IV**

THE BOSS MAN'S DAUGHTERS I II III IV V

A SAVAGE LOVE **I & II**

BAE BELONGS TO ME I II

A HUSTLER'S DECEIT I, II, III

WHAT BAD BITCHES DO I, II, III

SOUL OF A MONSTER I II III

KILL ZONE

A DOPE BOY'S QUEEN I II

By **Aryanna**

A KINGPIN'S AMBITON

A KINGPIN'S AMBITION **II**

I MURDER FOR THE DOUGH

By **Ambitious**

191

C.D. Blue

TRUE SAVAGE I II III IV V VI VII

DOPE BOY MAGIC I, II, III

MIDNIGHT CARTEL I II III

CITY OF KINGZ I II

By **Chris Green**

A DOPEBOY'S PRAYER

By **Eddie "Wolf" Lee**

THE KING CARTEL **I, II & III**

By **Frank Gresham**

THESE NIGGAS AIN'T LOYAL **I, II & III**

By **Nikki Tee**

GANGSTA SHYT **I II &III**

By **CATO**

THE ULTIMATE BETRAYAL

By **Phoenix**

BOSS'N UP **I , II & III**

By **Royal Nicole**

I LOVE YOU TO DEATH

By Destiny J

I RIDE FOR MY HITTA

I STILL RIDE FOR MY HITTA

By **Misty Holt**

LOVE & CHASIN' PAPER

By **Qay Crockett**

TO DIE IN VAIN

SINS OF A HUSTLA

By **ASAD**

BROOKLYN HUSTLAZ

By **Boogsy Morina**

BROOKLYN ON LOCK I & II

192

For the Love of a Boss

By **Sonovia**

GANGSTA CITY

By **Teddy Duke**

A DRUG KING AND HIS DIAMOND I & II III

A DOPEMAN'S RICHES

HER MAN, MINE'S TOO I, II

CASH MONEY HO'S

THE WIFEY I USED TO BE

By Nicole Goosby

TRAPHOUSE KING **I II & III**

KINGPIN KILLAZ I II III

STREET KINGS I II

PAID IN BLOOD **I II**

CARTEL KILLAZ I II III

DOPE GODS I II

By **Hood Rich**

LIPSTICK KILLAH **I, II, III**

CRIME OF PASSION I II & III

FRIEND OR FOE I II

By **Mimi**

STEADY MOBBN' **I, II, III**

THE STREETS STAINED MY SOUL

By **Marcellus Allen**

WHO SHOT YA **I, II, III**

SON OF A DOPE FIEND I II

Renta

GORILLAZ IN THE BAY **I II III IV**

TEARS OF A GANGSTA I II

3X KRAZY I II

DE'KARI

C.D. Blue

TRIGGADALE I II III

Elijah R. Freeman

GOD BLESS THE TRAPPERS I, II, III

THESE SCANDALOUS STREETS I, II, III

FEAR MY GANGSTA I, II, III IV, V

THESE STREETS DON'T LOVE NOBODY I, II

BURY ME A G I, II, III, IV, V

A GANGSTA'S EMPIRE I, II, III, IV

THE DOPEMAN'S BODYGAURD I II

THE REALEST KILLAZ I II III

THE LAST OF THE OGS

Tranay Adams

THE STREETS ARE CALLING

Duquie Wilson

MARRIED TO A BOSS... I II III

By Destiny Skai & Chris Green

KINGZ OF THE GAME I II III IV V

Playa Ray

SLAUGHTER GANG I II III

RUTHLESS HEART I II III

By Willie Slaughter

FUK SHYT

By Blakk Diamond

DON'T F#CK WITH MY HEART I II

By Linnea

ADDICTED TO THE DRAMA I II III

IN THE ARM OF HIS BOSS II

By Jamila

YAYO I II III IV

A SHOOTER'S AMBITION I II

For the Love of a Boss

By S. Allen

TRAP GOD I II III

By Troublesome

FOREVER GANGSTA

GLOCKS ON SATIN SHEETS I II

By Adrian Dulan

TOE TAGZ I II III

LEVELS TO THIS SHYT

By Ah'Million

KINGPIN DREAMS I II

By Paper Boi Rari

CONFESSIONS OF A GANGSTA I II III

By Nicholas Lock

I'M NOTHING WITHOUT HIS LOVE

SINS OF A THUG

By Monet Dragun

CAUGHT UP IN THE LIFE I II III

By Robert Baptiste

NEW TO THE GAME I II III

MONEY, MURDER & MEMORIES I II

By **Malik D. Rice**

LIFE OF A SAVAGE I II III

A GANGSTA'S QUR'AN I II III

MURDA SEASON I II III

GANGLAND CARTEL I II III

CHI'RAQ GANGSTAS I II

By **Romell Tukes**

LOYALTY AIN'T PROMISED I II

By Keith Williams

QUIET MONEY I II III

C.D. Blue

THUG LIFE I II

EXTENDED CLIP I II

By **Trai'Quan**

THE STREETS MADE ME I II

By **Larry D. Wright**

THE ULTIMATE SACRIFICE I, II, III, IV, V, VI

KHADIFI

IF YOU CROSS ME ONCE

ANGEL I II

By **Anthony Fields**

THE LIFE OF A HOOD STAR

By **Ca$h & Rashia Wilson**

THE STREETS WILL NEVER CLOSE

By **K'ajji**

CREAM

By **Yolanda Moore**

NIGHTMARES OF A HUSTLA I II

By **King Dream**

CONCRETE KILLAZ

By **Kingpen**

HARD AND RUTHLESS

By **Von Wiley Hall**

GHOST MOB II

Stilloan Robinson

MOB TIES

By **SayNoMore**

BODYMORE MURDERLAND

By **Delmont Player**

FOR THE LOVE OF A BOSS

By **C. D. Blue**

196

For the Love of a Boss

BOOKS BY LDP'S CEO, CA$H

TRUST IN NO MAN

TRUST IN NO MAN 2

TRUST IN NO MAN 3

BONDED BY BLOOD

SHORTY GOT A THUG

THUGS CRY

THUGS CRY 2

THUGS CRY 3

TRUST NO BITCH

TRUST NO BITCH 2

TRUST NO BITCH 3

TIL MY CASKET DROPS

RESTRAINING ORDER

RESTRAINING ORDER 2

IN LOVE WITH A CONVICT

LIFE OF A HOOD STAR

C.D. Blue

CPSIA information can be obtained
at www.ICGtesting.com
Printed in the USA
LVHW051709190421
684911LV00011B/1347